Come Back to Me

Annie Seaton

Love Across Time: Book 1

Follow Me: Book 2
Finding Home: Book 3
The Threads that Bind: Book 4

DEDICATION

This book is dedicated to Kate and Dane, our talented children, who both inherited the family music gene.

ACKNOWLEDGEMENT

In memory of David Bowie, who wrote *Starman*, the song that began my lifelong love affair with his music. His music has given me so much happiness over the years, and inspired this story where Davy Morgan wrote his own songs.

David Bowie R.I.P
1947-2016
"He was an extraordinary man, full of love and life. He will always be with us. For now, it is appropriate to cry."

Toni Visconti
BBC news
11 January 2016

Chapter One

Megan Miller ignored the strident ring of the telephone on her desk. It was the sixth time it had rung in the past half hour and she'd managed to ignore all the calls, but it was impossible to ignore the determined knocking on her door.

No time. The final three student assessment tasks were queued on her screen waiting to be marked, and in two hours she had to be at the airport to catch the late afternoon Qantas flight to London.

Whoever it was would have to wait.

The phone stopped and there was blessed silence for a couple of minutes but she knew it was too good to last. Megan rolled her eyes as the knocking on her office door continued.

"Megan!" The voice of Beth McLaren, her teaching colleague and best friend came through the closed door. "Megan, I know you're in there."

Sighing, Megan pushed her chair back and stood. It looked like the last bit of marking would have to wait until she got to Glastonbury *if* there was internet access in the cottage where she was staying. Or maybe she could mark at the airport while she waited to board her flight. The last thing she wanted to worry about when she left on the trip she'd dreamed of for years was marking assessment tasks from students with appalling literacy skills. Her fail rate was too high this semester and she'd already been told she had to pass more students.

Crossing the room, she opened the door just as Beth was about to knock again.

"What the heck have you been doing?" Beth grabbed her arm and pushed her back into her office. Students walking along the corridor of the sociology department shot them curious looks.

"I've been trying to ring you for the last half hour, but your mobile goes straight to voicemail. I had to run across from the main administration building to find you."

"Where's the fire?" Megan slipped her old cardigan over her shoulders. She'd dressed for comfort on the plane before she'd left home with her luggage this morning and knew she looked more like a student than a lecturer at the prestigious university in Sydney. "Beth, do you know if there is internet in your aunt's cottage? I haven't—"

"Megan. For goodness' sake, listen to me! The vice chancellor and the board have been waiting"— Beth glanced at her watch— "for over half an hour for you to turn up at the meeting." She ran her fingers through her short-cropped auburn hair. "You have to get over to the board room *now*."

"What meeting?" Megan was mystified. She had no knowledge of any meeting she was expected to attend. Excitement curled in her stomach until she looked down at her bright red jeans and white T-shirt. "Oh, no. I've been waiting for weeks to hear about the promotion and of course it had to happen today of all days." She'd been filling in as senior lecturer for a semester, and the successful permanent appointee was about to be announced.

Beth shook her head. "I don't think so. His secretary called me. She was looking for you, and then she asked me if I was going to be your support person."

"Support person? Why a support person?" Megan frowned and her heart rate notched up a beat. "I haven't got time for this today. I'm flying to London, remember?" If there was one thing that she hated it was being late for anything. Being on time was one of her personal quirks—her mum and dad had always laughed at her adherence to schedules and appointments; it was not a trait inherited from a couple of music-loving hippies.

And that made this day even worse: the tasks weren't going to get marked by the deadline, she was going to be late getting to the airport, and worst of all, she'd missed some sort of important meeting.

Being late for anything stressed Megan out.

Big time.

"Apparently, you were sent a letter. 'Cankle Nancy' was most specific, beneath that holier-than-us attitude she always has. She was positively smirking that you hadn't turned up." The 'Cankle Nancy' nickname was a private one coined by Beth and Megan who were invariably treated with rude disdain by the VC's secretary. Ms Robinson suffered from swollen ankles that spilled over her shoes.

"She's a cow, that's for sure, but I have no idea what this meeting is for." Megan hurried across to her desk and picked up the pile of unopened letters that had sat there for the past week. Her marking load had been horrendous while she'd filled in the temporary position and she'd had no time for the daily administration tasks. Even senior lecturers didn't qualify for secretarial assistance. Anything important—and meeting notices and minutes—usually came through the university email.

"Why couldn't they have emailed me?" she muttered under her breath when she found a white envelope embossed with 'Professor Roger Devine, Vice Chancellor, North Shore University' along the top edge. "That's how they usually communicate."

She turned the letter over curiously wondering what it was all about. It looked very official.

"For goodness' sake, Megs, open it." Beth put her hand on Megan's arm. "They're all waiting over there, and Nancy said to get you there quick smart."

Megan ripped it open and scanned the contents and her stomach lurched. "What the—?"

"What? What does it say?"

"Ring Nancy and tell her I'm on my way." Megan shook off Beth's hand and strode around to the other side of her desk and reached into her bag. Glancing down at her phone, she flicked it off silent and grimaced as she saw the list of calls she'd missed over the past half hour. She blocked out the sound of Beth's voice as she pressed hash and nine, the shortcut to her brother-in-law's mobile.

"Please be there, Tony. Please be there." She closed her eyes as she muttered. A chill had taken hold of her and she used her free hand to pull her cardigan tightly around her chest.

The phone picked up immediately and before her brother-in-law could speak, Megan interrupted.

"Tony, are you on campus?"

"Yes," he replied. "What's up? I thought you were leaving—"

Megan cut him off. "I need you as a support person in a meeting. Right now. Meet me at the VC's boardroom. I'll explain when you get there."

"I'm on my way."

Having a lawyer in the family had been handy when her parents had died last year. As well as dealing with the tragedy, and sorting out the family house, Megan and her sister, Kathy, had to sort out the mess of their estate. Tony, Kathy's husband, worked part-time at his family's law firm, but his first love was academia and now he spent most of his time at the university lecturing in his associate professorial position

Beth's voice interrupted her thoughts. "Megan, please tell me. What the hell is going on?"

Megan picked up the letter and was surprised to see the fine paper shaking in her hand. Taking a deep breath, she read the first paragraph to her friend.

"As you have not responded in writing to the allegations made against you, you are required to appear before the disciplinary committee at one pm, Thursday the seventeenth of June, 2011."

"Disciplinary committee? And what allegations?"

Quickly skimming the rest of the letter, she looked up at Beth and shook her head. "I have no idea. It doesn't say. And I've had no other communication about any allegations, either in a meeting or by email or letter."

Megan picked up the rest of the unopened mail and discarded the letters one by one as she flicked through them. "Nothing else. That's all there is."

Beth grabbed her hand. "Come on, I'll walk over with you."

"I can't go like this." Megan gestured to her clothes and purple Doc Martens. "I look like a radical student, not a serious sociology lecturer." She glanced over at her suitcase by the door, all packed and waiting for the taxi she'd booked to take her from the North Shore to Sydney International Airport at two thirty. "I've got decent clothes in my luggage. I'll have to change."

"Megs, you haven't got time. You'll have to come like that. Now, come on." Beth pulled her across to the door and Megan threw her faded cardigan on the chair before they stepped into the corridor.

Nancy Robinson glared at her over the top of her thick spectacles as Megan walked into the foyer of the board room, flanked by her best friend and her brother-in-law. "You're very late for the meeting, Miss Miller." Her voice was cold—but her expression was filled with satisfaction at Megan's tardiness.

Bitch.

Megan looked at the woman who had always treated her with dislike. Her eyes were protruding, and the large pouchy bags beneath them gave her a permanent hangdog expression. She looked like one of those cartoon characters with the permanent whine.

Biting back the retort hovering on her lips, Megan smiled even though her face felt as though it would crack from the effort. "My sincerest apologies, Miss Robinson. I haven't had a chance to clear my snail mail,"— she emphasized the word s*nail*— "and as you know this has been a marking week. An email or an internal network message would have found me much more reliably. Perhaps next time you could use that." She kept her tone even and saccharine-sweet.

The secretary looked at her primly, her thin lips pursed before she spoke. "Some processes are too formal for email, Miss Miller. And I doubt if there will be a next time. Your case is very serious indeed."

Tony stepped with a brisk nod. "I think you are breaching confidentiality there, Nancy. I don't believe it is your business—or your place—to comment."

Miss Robinson coloured brick-red as she glared at them. "I will call the *disciplinary* committee and advise them of your arrival." She looked Megan up and down as she picked up the telephone on her desk. The curl of her lip said it all as she took in Megan's attire.

After speaking into the telephone, she turned to Tony. "Professor Gaines, you and Miss Miller may go in now."

Beth reached over and hugged Megan. "I'll wait out here while this mess is sorted out. God knows, whatever it is, it's the last thing you need after the last six months."

Chapter Two

The accident that changed Megan's life happened on a lazy Sunday afternoon in late spring, 2010. Her parents had been on their way back to Sydney from a deceased estate sale in the lower Blue Mountains.

"Your father's found a sale with old sheet music and vinyl records going back to the fifties." Mum had sounded less than enthusiastic when she'd called that morning, but she always kept Dad company on his jaunts to whatever sale was going. "But I think there's a Christmas artisan market at Faulconbridge today too, so it won't be too boring."

"Pick me up some creamed honey if you see some, please, Mum," Megan had asked.

"I will, love."

Megan still carried guilt brought on by the last words her mother ever spoke to her. "Dad said there's something there that you'll love, that's why we're going so far today. Consider it an early Christmas present. We'll call in for a drink on the way home."

"Stay for dinner too. Tony's promised homemade pizzas tonight in the wood fire." Megan lived in a granny flat underneath Kathy and Tony's house. "And you know what a gourmet cook he is." Megan remembered laughing about Kathy's cooking skills. "Just as well, poor Kath can't even boil water without setting the smoke alarm off."

"We'll be there for sure. See you later." Mum had said.

But there was no later.

They'd held dinner off until nine o'clock waiting for them to arrive but neither she nor Kathy had been particularly worried. They'd even joked that Dad had treated Mum to a romantic night in the mountains. A niggle of concern had taken root when both of their phones had gone to voicemail when Kathy had called to see if they were still coming for dinner, but they assumed that they were either out of range or more likely had switched them off.

"Stupid technology," Dad had grumbled. "If I want to talk to someone I'll call them when I get home. I don't need a phone on me all day long."

Megan had gone back downstairs after they'd finished the pizza, and was about to go to bed when Kathy had come running down to her flat.

"Quick, put your television on. Oh, God, Megan. I saw their car. I'm sure it's theirs." Her face was white and her voice was shaking.

If it hadn't been for the original vinyl copy of Davy Morgan's last album that had been in the boot of Mum and Dad's car—along with the promised jar of creamed honey Megan doubted if they would have travelled to the sale that day.

No matter how many times Kathy told her she wasn't to blame, Megan carried the guilt that if it hadn't been for that album, and her obsession with collecting seventies memorabilia—especially anything to do with Davy Morgan—
her parents wouldn't have been involved in the accident. An out-of-control petrol tanker had caused carnage on the highway when its brakes failed.
It had been their parents' distinctive BMW that Kathy had seen on the news. The back from the rear seat was intact, including their shopping spoils from the day. The damage to the front—Megan blocked that sight from her memory—had made it impossible for anyone to survive.

The following few months had been horrendous. As Kathy and Megan tried to pack up the house, and sort their parents' possessions, Megan was offered a temporary contract as a senior lecturer at the university and her face-to-face lecture hours increased, along with the time spent in lecture preparation and marking. Research was put on the back burner, until she couldn't leave her doctoral thesis any longer.

Kathy spiralled into depression, and Megan—with Beth's help—had tried to support her. Not only was she not coping with the tragedy, she and Tony were in the middle of their last attempt at IVF.

Megan did the best she could—although her relationship with her only sibling had always been fraught with arguments. Her own mental health suffered, but she buried herself in work determined not to give in.

"You have to eat." Beth turned up at her office door every day and dragged her off to the university staff house for lunch. If it hadn't been for Beth, Megan was sure she would have walked away from the university. Poor Beth had her own problems—she was in the middle of a messy divorce—and as summer faded into a dreary and bleak autumn, Megan wondered if any of them would ever be happy again.
One thing she had decided, she was going to forgo her planned research trip to Glastonbury in the UK summer because she didn't want to leave Kathy while she was so fragile. She kept putting off booking the tickets, and was about to cancel the leave she'd applied for.

In March, five months after the accident, Megan was marking—as usual. Surely she would finish soon. Davy Morgan's '*Come Back to Me*' was playing softly in the background on her computer, and a measure of calm stole over her for the first time in many weeks.

She'd jumped as a knock sounded at her door, and pressed pause on the music program.

"Who is it?" she called.

"It's me. Kathy."

Megan widened her eyes as she opened the door. Kathy's hair was newly cut and she had a touch of lipstick on, and she was wearing a pretty dress, and a long white cardigan.

"Come in." Megan held the door open and stood back as her sister stepped through. "You look... good," she said carefully.

Kathy's smile was wide. "I have something to tell you. Two things, actually."

"Tell me?" Megan frowned and pulled her old cardigan close around her. The autumn had been cold and she wasn't looking forward to winter.

"You're the second to know." Kath spoke quickly, her words running together as she reached for Megan's hands. "You had to know next. After Tony."

"Know what?"

Kathy's hands were warm as they gripped Megan's cold fingers. Since Mum and Dad had died, she'd lost weight and it was hard to keep warm.

"We're pregnant. It worked, Megs. We're going to have a baby."

Megan closed her eyes as the little tendrils of happiness she'd felt for many weeks unfurled in her chest. She couldn't help the tears that threatened to spill over as she held onto the warm, unfamiliar feeling.

"Oh my God!" She grabbed Kathy and hugged her. "Oh, Kath, sweetie, I'm so happy for you. Both of you. How far along are you?"

"We didn't want to jinx our chances by telling anyone. I'm almost four months."

The tears spilled over in earnest now. "Oh, Kath. Mum and Dad would have been so happy."

"I know they would. But it's time to move on. They'd both want us to celebrate life."

"I know. Wherever they are, they're together, and that's what's kept me going." Megan sniffed and turned away. She didn't know whether to smile or cry but Kath grabbed her hand again.

"I want you to know how much I've appreciated you being there for me over the past few months. I've been hard to deal with, I know, but it's been just as hard for you, but I've leaned on you—and Tony so much."

"It's been tough for all of us. But let's see this as a turning point. For all of us."

"It is. And you've got it. It's for a*ll* of us." Kathy reached into the deep pocket of her cardigan and pulled out a blue plastic wallet. "But this is for you by yourself. To say thank you. From both of us, Tony and me."

Megan frowned as Kathy put the plastic wallet into her hand. "What is it?"

"A business class return ticket to the UK. We've booked it for you. I know you were talking about cancelling your trip and your leave but there's no need to. Tony said your temp contract is up the week before we booked your flight, and Beth has organised for you to stay in her family's cottage in Glastonbury. You'll be there just in time for the festival."

"Oh no. I can't go. I can't accept this." Megan shook her head.

"Yes, you can. Not only are you going to be an aunty, you're going to Glastonbury."

Kathy's happy smile was worth it as Megan gave in.

She grabbed her sister and danced her around the room. "Oh my God. I am. I'm going to Glastonbury!"

Megan looked at the ticket in her hand, and her smile grew as wide as Kathy's.

Chapter Three

Tony preceded Megan into the board room. The only sound was the hum of the air conditioning and she wished she'd left her cardigan on. The room was freezing and the faces of the five men sitting around the large table were as icy as the air in the large room.

"Come in." The vice chancellor stood and gestured for them to take the two remaining vacant seats at the table. "Professor Gaines, I am assuming you are Miss Miller's support person?"

"That is correct." Tony squeezed Megan's hand before taking the seat next to her. The unfamiliar man on her left poured two glasses of water from the jug in the middle of the table and placed one in front of each of them.

Megan looked up but neither of her sociology colleagues would meet her gaze. The professor in charge of her department sat to the right of the vice-chancellor and her unit co-ordinator sat on his left. They both looked down at the papers in front of them and shuffled through the pages as though their lives depended on it.

The financial bursar of the university met her gaze and he didn't hold her eye for long either.

Tony leaned forward and directed a question to the vice-chancellor. "What the hell is this all about, Roger?"

The vice-chancellor pushed a single piece of paper across to Tony. "You are familiar with the role of the support person, of course, Professor?"

"Yes, of course I am." Tony's voice was irritable as he turned to Megan. "The role of a support person is to ensure you are treated fairly, and I'm not allowed to speak unless you become distressed and I request a break for you."

Megan shook her head and tried to keep her voice confident. "Why would I get upset? I have no idea why I am here." She looked down at her watch. "If you are unaware of my plans, I'm on leave from lunchtime and I have an international flight to catch in less than three hours." Her voice shook and her chest ached with the effort of holding her anger and frustration in check. If there was one thing she hated it was being out of control. Her emotions were in a fragile enough state from the events of the past few months. "So can we get started please?" She swallowed and took a deep breath waiting to hear what the problem was. Whatever it was she'd been accused of. On the way over to the building Megan had racked her brains but still had no idea what this meeting was about.

"Miss Miller, three weeks ago, a letter of allegation was sent to you with some serious concerns about your behaviour in your role as acting senior lecturer in the sociology department. You were given fourteen days to respond in writing. As you have not responded, that has been taken as an admission that the allegations are correct and you are not interested in disputing them. Today, the disciplinary board will hand down their decision and the consequence."

Tony looked at Megan before turning back to the vice-chancellor. "I request a break for Miss Miller."

"Now?" The vice chancellor frowned

"No." Megan stood and placed her hands firmly on the edge of the table before glancing across at her brother-in-law. "I don't want a bloody break. I want to know what this is all about and to get to the bottom of it now. I've received no such letter. This is the first I've heard of this garbage."

"Please watch your language and sit down, Miss Miller. If you don't require a break, we will continue."

Megan sat back down and folded her arms across her chest. The hard chair pressed through her thin T-shirt and she concentrated on keeping her back straight as she held the gaze of the vice-chancellor.

He nodded to one of the men she didn't recognise. "You may begin."

The man opened a folder and began to read. Disbelief vied with anger as Megan listened to the words.

"Allegation number one: it is alleged Miss Miller has falsified marks in the university grade centre system in exchange for financial recompense. Allegation number two: it is alleged that her upcoming overseas trip has been funded in exchange for the granting of a High Distinction to a student in the sociology department. Allegation number three: it is alleged—"

"Stop right there." Tony pushed his chair back. "My wife and I paid for Megan's overseas trip and I can prove that with little problem."

"Allegation number three, it is alleged—"

"That is garbage!" Megan's voice rang out over the table as she jumped to her feet and her chair fell back against the wall. She ignored the glares from the men sitting across the table. "It's a pack of lies. Absolute lies."

"Please sit down, Miss Miller. Once more and we will close the meeting."

What the hell were they on about?

Tony's hand on her arm brought Megan back to a semblance of calm. The room was spinning and a red haze filled her vision. She swallowed the nausea that was building in her chest and closed her eyes for a second to regain her balance.

Opening her eyes, she turned to the vice-chancellor and lowered her voice.

"Professor Devine, I apologise for my outburst. However, none of this is true. There can't be any evidence because it's simply not true." Megan fought to stop the trembling of her chin. "This is the first I have heard of such...lies. And that is the reason I haven't responded."

"Please wait till the allegations are read in their entirety, Miss Miller."

"There's more?"

Tony reached over and held her hand as twelve more allegations of inappropriate behaviour were levelled against her. Allegations of misappropriation of funds, inappropriate relationships with students, fudging marks, impolite interactions with staff and the list went on...and on.

And there was more to come. The final allegation that she had plagiarised material for her doctorate finally brought her undone.

"You cannot be bloody serious?" Megan slammed her hands on the table and her water glass went flying.

She stood and watched, bemused as water trickled across the table towards the vice-chancellor. Before the water reached his papers, he snatched them off the table, and then gestured to the man beside him to deal with the mess.

A surreal feeling washed over Megan as she watched the water drip from the table.

Drip by drip. Almost in slow motion. She wanted to pinch herself.

Am I dreaming? Nothing that had been said was anywhere near the truth. The only person in the sociology department she'd ever had words with was another lecturer and—

Of course. That was it!

"Greg Cannon. It was Greg Cannon, wasn't it?" Certainty overtook her disbelief and she squared her shoulders as the water was mopped up from the table with paper towel. "He has been doing everything he can to make me look bad in meetings because he wanted the promotion that I'm in line for. He was upset when I was appointed to the relieving position. It's Greg Cannon who has made these vexatious allegations!"

"Miss Miller, this is your last warning. Please sit down immediately or this meeting will conclude now." The vice chancellor glared at her. "We have documentary evidence of your wrongdoing and your most unprofessional behaviour today is simply confirming that the allegations are correct."

Tony pulled her back down into her chair and leaned across to whisper in her ear. "Calm down, Meg. We'll sort this out. You're not doing yourself any favours by reacting like this."

The voices and the horrid words droned around her for another five minutes until the final words of the vice-chancellor caught her attention.

"All allegations have been upheld. The other parties involved have been interviewed and there is incontrovertible evidence of guilt." The vice-chancellor stood and looked down at Megan. "Miss Miller, you are hereby dismissed from your temporary contract at North Shore University and will be escorted from the premises immediately."

As Megan's world fell to pieces around her, one of the other men who she hadn't recognised stood and came around to stand behind her.

"Security will accompany you to your office while you collect your belongings."

"Don't I get to speak? Why don't I get interviewed? I need to show you all of this is untrue." Megan knew her voice was rising to a screech but her absolute distress— and the unfairness and untruth— of the allegations were drowning her. She knew the tears rolling down her cheeks would be seen as an admission of guilt but she couldn't stop them. It was as though she was in a parallel universe watching from outside of reality. "I can answer any questions that you've got. Ask me, I'll answer anything now."

Her trip to London was the least of her worries at the moment. She had to get out of this mess. It was ironic; Megan knew her ethics were of the highest standard. She was so honest, she didn't even take the reams of photocopy paper out of the cupboard without getting permission from 'Cankle Nancy', let alone fudge marks or take a bribe. The allegations were ridiculous and anyone who knew her would know that.

Her heart sank as she thought of the rest of the staff. Nancy seemed to know all about this. How many other people in the university had heard these stories and believed them?

"You now have a seven-day appeal period, Miss Miller. This meeting is concluded and a transcript of the minutes will be sent to your home address. "Your access to the university network, and your email account, have been withdrawn."

Tony took her arm and led her from the room, followed by the security man. Beth waited in the foyer and her face was blurred as Megan looked at her through tears.

"Beth, this can't be happening?" Megan put shaking hands over her face as she choked back another sob. "This is so not true."

"What's happened?" Beth put her arm around Megan's shoulder. "What was it all about?"

Tony shook his head. "Not now. Beth. Not here." He glared over at Nancy who was watching them with the same smug smile on her face. "We have to go to Megan's office now and get her stuff and then we'll all go for a coffee and work this ridiculous situation out."

Reality intruded on Megan's distress and she tried to look at her watch but couldn't see the digital screen through her tears. Her whole body was shaking and she dug in her pocket for a tissue and dabbed at her eyes with shaking fingers.

"What time is it?" Her voice appeared to be coming from someone else. Cotton wool fuzziness filled her head and her lips were moving but she had trouble finding the words she wanted. "The...taxi is...getting...picking me up for the airport...soon... at two thirty."

"I'll cancel it. I'll drive you over. Kath was meeting you there to see you off, wasn't she?" Beth said.

"But I can't go now. I'll have to cancel the trip. I have to stay and fight this. I have to." Megan's stomach clenched, and disappointment flooded through her as the prospect of her trip disappeared. "I'm not going. Just take me home."

Tony spoke to her quietly as the security guard led them towards the Social Sciences building. "No Meg, you can't cancel your trip. I'll get this sorted out while you're away."

"But I've only got seven days to appeal." Megan swallowed another sob. "I got so bloody emotional it looked like I was guilty. You know it's not true, don't you, Tony?"

Tony stopped in front of her and tipped her face up to meet his serious gaze. The feel of his firm fingers on her chin grounded her and her confusion dissipated a little. His brown eyes always exuded calm and serenity. He was a great partner for Kath; he provided a steady counter to her personality. Megan still wondered how they'd ended up together but they seemed so happy, and Tony had slotted into the family well. And now he was going to be a father too.

"Of course I do. Anyone who knows you can see it's a setup. But if you don't appeal and have it overturned, you'll never get a job in another university and no one else will take you on as a doctoral student."

"That's why I can't get on the plane." Megan shook her head as her voice caught. She was stuck between a rock and a hard place. "But if I don't go on this trip, I'll never have the opportunity again. The Stones are playing at Glastonbury next week and I've waited for the opportunity to do a Glastonbury Festival for years."

Anger overtook her confused thoughts as determination filled her.

She set off again with long angry strides towards her office. "It's all bullshit and I can prove that Greg Cannon is behind every malicious allegation. I'm going to front him right now."

Beth raised her eyebrows. Megan rarely swore, or raised her voice.

Tony hurried along behind her and caught her arm. "Calm down, Megan. I know how you're feeling but you have to step back and let the process happen."

"You can't know. I'm the one who's been accused. I knew Greg was up to something. That bloody man weaselled his way into my bed, and he was way too interested in everything I was doing at work." Megan gritted her teeth as her suspicions fell into place. "He wanted that promotion and I was a certainty over him."

"So why do you think Greg's responsible?"

"I thought it was strange a few weeks ago when my log-in and password wouldn't work. They've been fine for three years. He obviously got hold of them and logged in as me and changed marks or something."

"I'll ask the IT department for a login audit." Tony's voice held the first shred of hope she'd heard so far.

"He's smart enough to have covered his tracks, but I suppose it's worth a try if you think they'll do one."

"Whatever we do, we have to follow the procedures for you to have any chance for an appeal." His voice was quiet and calm.

"Huh, and look what that 'process' has done so far? I didn't know anything about it and I've been tried and found guilty without any procedural fairness. I got no letter." Megan kept walking despite Tony taking her arm.

Beth and Tony flanked her on either side as she strode through the building to her office, the security man hurrying to keep up with them. By the time she'd retrieved her suitcase, her bag and her laptop and the few personal possessions the security man would allow her to take from the top drawer of her desk, a small measure of calm had stolen over her.

It's all lies and I can prove that with little trouble.

It was hard to believe that someone would go to such lengths to discredit her. She'd gotten through the tragedy of losing her parents last year and this situation was nowhere near as bad. It was all malicious lies, paperwork and bureaucratic bullshit and she would deal with it. It was a job, but it wasn't the end of the world. She *had* to deal with it.

And I will.

If there was one thing it was going to do, it was going to make her take a bit more notice of what was happening around her. Megan knew she buried herself away; she was more than happy in her own company. Losing herself in her music as she worked had helped her get through the horror of last year.

As the security man locked the office door behind her, she stood in the corridor and bit her lip.

She *could* trust Tony to do the appeal. She could keep in touch by Skype, and if she was required at any further meetings, she could Skype that too. Hopefully, by the time she came back from her month in the United Kingdom it would be sorted. She squared her shoulders; she wasn't going to let this impact her trip. She would catch her flight this afternoon. The research on the sociological aspects of the Glastonbury music event over thirty years was the final step towards her doctorate.

It would all get sorted.

It would.

If it didn't, she'd deal with that when it happened.

Kathy and Megan were very different in appearance and personality. Megan had always been the academic one, and Kathy constantly told her she had her head in the clouds.

"There's real life out there. Get your nose out of the dusty books," Kathy would say. She was brash and loud, and didn't trust easily, and when her sister had fallen for Tony, Megan had paid out on her in bucket loads.

Where Kathy was petite, fair-skinned and blonde—she always said it was her size that made her stand up for herself, Megan was tall and auburn-haired with olive skin. Burying her nose in books as a child, while Kathy had excelled at every sport she'd taken on, had isolated Megan, and confidence had always been a problem for her.

"I'm pleased you've decided to go on your trip. You know you can trust me to appeal and to do it properly?" Tony looked across the table at Megan as Kathy held her hand. Beth had stood behind her since they had ordered their coffee in the departure terminal at the airport. Now she rubbed Megan's back in soothing circles.

The support of her family and best friend was going to get her through this. The problem was going to be the distance, but knowing Kath she'd call every day if she knew Megan needed her.

"Absolutely, Tony. You know I trust you. All the paperwork you'll need is in folders in my study at the flat. That can answer the financial and marking allegations. And you've got the credit card records for paying for my ticket, haven't you? The others I'll have to deal with personally." She turned to Kathy. "Do you know where your key to the flat is?"

Her sister nodded and Megan continued. "Any questions you've got, email me and I'll sort them out. If they propose a meeting before I'm home, they'll just have to wait till August. If they won't wait, I'll go higher. I'll even go to the media if I have to." She stared at her brother-in-law. "I need to see the letter so I can look at all of the allegations in detail. It'll all work out because I haven't done anything wrong."

Tony dropped his head in his hands. "Megan, you are such a Pollyanna. If there is a political move to get you out, they will, no matter what evidence you can produce."

She shook her head. "But I've done nothing wrong."

"It doesn't matter. The system can be corrupt and if there is a hidden motive for them to get you out, they will win. Don't expect that there will be any integrity or justice, just because you're innocent." He held her gaze and uncertainty filled her for the first time since they'd decided on the plan of attack. "And believe me, I have seen some unfair decisions over the years. Okay, I'll word up an appeal and lodge it for you. If I have any questions, I'll email you."

Beth leaned forward. "Megs, there's no internet in Violet Cottage. In fact, Aunt Alice wouldn't even have a phone connected. You'll have to go into the village to the public phone. Reverse the charges so you don't have to worry about old-fashioned call cards or coins."

"Don't worry, I'll sort something out. I'm sure there'll be an internet café or something. You just get the appeal organised and do whatever has to be done." Megan turned away from Tony and looked at Beth. "I'm so grateful to your family for letting me stay in your aunt's cottage. Now I just have to find my way there."

"You can catch the train from Paddington station to Castle Cary. There'll be buses to the festival but if you grab a taxi at the station, you'll be able to go straight to Violet Cottage."

Megan looked from her best friend to Tony and Kathy, the only family she had left, and tears filled her eyes.

"You look after my new little niece or nephew, Kath."

As her sister hugged her, Megan knew they'd be there for her no matter what, and once she came home, she'd show them how much she appreciated their support. She'd be the best damn babysitter there was.

Now it was time to say goodbye and make her way to the boarding gate and try to stay calm and focus on her research.

This whole stuff up could mean the end of her career and she was determined to fight it. The timing sucked but she would come back and sort it out in a month. She would try to switch off as best she could, enjoy the festival, get her research data and try to block this from her mind until she came home. Learning to meditate had helped her block unwanted thoughts last year when she'd been trying to work, and cope with the grief of her parents' deaths; she'd do it again.

Now she had this opportunity to achieve her dream and visit Glastonbury, that sneaky, lying lowlife who wanted her job was not going to take it from her.

Chapter Four

Megan snapped her laptop shut as the captain announced they were only half an hour out of Heathrow Airport. The second leg of the long-haul flight from Dubai had passed quickly, and she'd organised all of her notes and files ready to begin her research at Glastonbury. A shiver of anticipation rippled through her as she realised that in less than an hour her feet would be on the ground in England, and her lifetime dreams were about to be achieved— visiting England, going to a music festival, and experiencing the British music scene firsthand.

The screen on the back of the seat beside her caught her attention and she leaned forward with interest as the credits for a seventies music show ran down the screen. She flicked her own TV on, slipped the earphones over her ears and scrolled through the music programs. She found and selected the seventies show and grinned when Davy Morgan strutted onto the stage.

How good was that? Megan had spent the past hour reading about him and now she could listen to his music…and watch him. It didn't get much better than that. The librarian at the university had e-mailed the final articles scanned from the old microfiche copies of *It's Here and Now*, the music magazine from the seventies that Megan was using for some of her research. The article was one she hadn't read before and the photograph had caught her attention. It was the same photograph as the poster she'd had up on her wall when she was a teenager. The lurid headline hinted at a scandal but she ignored it. Her research had shown that scandals for rock stars in the seventies were manufactured on a daily basis to boost record sales.

And the media hadn't changed much. In those days, the gossip had been in print. With today's social media, a rock star couldn't sneeze without it being tweeted or Instagrammed immediately.

Megan had been fascinated by the seventies music loved by her parents, and she'd preferred it over the nineties bands her friends had followed. Her fascination with the era had continued through university, and now formed the basis of her doctorate. Her research on Davy Morgan had come to a dead end soon after 1971. It seemed besides a few tours in late '71 and early '72, he'd become a bit of a recluse and there was very little information on him, apart from his appearance at the Glastonbury festivals for a few years after that, and reviews of his later albums. It was as though he'd disappeared…the only mention of him was a rumor that he'd retired to an island somewhere to write his music.

Megan reached over and turned the volume up and closed her eyes as Davy sang "For Megan." She'd always loved that song; when she'd been a teenager, she'd imagined he'd written it for her. She knew it had been a factor in her fascination with Davy Morgan's music.

Come back to me, Megan.

Together we will conquer time.

It had been the beginning of a journey that was now culminating in the final research for her doctorate on the sociology of seventies music and festivals. She couldn't help the grin that she knew was spreading across her face.

Megan Miller was going to go to her first Glastonbury festival.

She was in England.

After they'd landed and Megan had collected her luggage, made her way through customs, and had her passport scanned, she found a quiet corner and pulled out her mobile phone. It took a couple of minutes to locate a provider but eventually, she had service…and fifteen text messages.

What the hell? They were all from Kathy, and her stomach clenched as she thought the worst.

Oh gosh. Not the baby, please.

Rather than pick up the messages, she dialled her sister's number and she picked up on the first ring.

"Megan, you're there?"

"Yeah, what's so urgent?"

"I just wanted to know how you are now that you've arrived. Did you get any sleep? Are you calmer now?"

"Good, yes, and yes." Megan smiled as she looked around her. "I'm happy, and I'm calm. You worried me, I thought there was something wrong. Now let me step outside into England and enjoy myself. I'll call you in the morning after I get down to Beth's family's place."

Megan wondered if she'd been foolish leaving the country while Tony handled the appeal. Could she trust that she'd be treated fairly? Would everything be sorted by the time she went home? The research for her doctorate on the Glastonbury music event over thirty years was the final step towards her thesis and she couldn't afford to give up the opportunity. But the flip side was: if she stayed and was found guilty, the research would be for nothing. If she did lose her job at the university, she'd never get another academic job anywhere else.

This whole mess could mean the end of her career and her doctorate. The timing sucked, but she would fight it. For now, she would try to focus on Glastonbury as best she could, get her research data, enjoy the festival, and try to block out the appeal until she went home. It was in Tony's capable hands.

Megan put the phone into her pocket and grabbed the handle on her suitcase. She looked down at purple Doc Martins and smiled as disbelief ran through her. Her feet were actually on English soil.

Chapter Five

"Shit."

David Morgan hitched his guitar up on his shoulder and cursed for the second time that night. The band practice session had gone late because the pyramid stage had been only half set up when they'd gotten to Worthy Farm in Pilton at midday. The organisers had tried to find the best site by using a witching rod so they could set the stage above the magical ley line that was supposed to run through here from Stonehenge. It was said to be lucky.

David strode across the field trying to shake off the anger that consumed him. Everything had gone wrong today. Bear, their drummer, had been late because of the crowds gawking at the musicians along the road into the farm. Someone had let slip that Bowie and the Stones were rehearsing, and everyone had come to the festival site hoping to see them. By the time he and the band had set up and rehearsed, it had been pitch dark despite almost being midsummer.

If they'd asked *him* where to put the stage, he could have shown them straight up. But he was not in the mood to talk to anyone. Holly Love, their publicist, had handed him the latest issue of the *Taunton Times* and he'd thrown it onto the stage floor in disgust when he'd read the bullshit the journalist had written up about how his band was about to break up because of some torrid fling he was supposed to have had with Bear's girlfriend. Jesus, Bear didn't even have a woman at the moment. Anything to sell a magazine or newspaper.

It had taken David three attempts to get back home across the fields and by the time he got there he was royally pissed off. He'd spent an hour wandering around in the dark before he'd finally found the stones and made his way across to the back garden of Rose Cottage. Someone had been there before him, because the small front gate leading to the narrow laneway was open.

No matter how much he protected his privacy and tried to hide, some groupie always managed to find him.

No matter where, or *when* he was.

After the first festival, he'd moved down to Glastonbury and settled into a vacant cottage outside the village to take refuge from the publicity and the journalists who constantly chased him. Music had flowed, and he had written new songs, day and night. Alice McLaren lived next door and she'd shown him the way to his future. At first, he'd been sceptical, but the day she'd taken him to the standing stones, a new world had opened up for him—an opportunity to escape the relentless pursuit of the press—and he had embraced it.

When Alice had first told him about the ley line behind the cottages, he'd thought it was just her new age hippie ramblings, but she'd taken him over to the three large markers in the field. She'd placed his hands on the bluish-gray stone. He'd jumped back as they'd hummed and moved beneath his fingers. The next day he'd gone exploring alone, and had slipped through to the future for the first time. When he'd come back, Alice had explained it. Her family had been travelling through the time gate for centuries. Listening to her explanation of ley lines and time slips had fascinated him.

Carefully, he'd explored the future—his future. It was as though he'd come home, taking him away from all the obsessed fans and groupies who constantly followed his band, or *any* band. When he had discovered how successful he'd been in the seventies, and the wealth he'd accrued since then, it had almost done his head in. The day he went up to London and recognised the elderly banker—who was still the same man who'd set up his accounts in 1972—everything had fallen into place for him. Clive was the only other person, apart from Alice and the guys in the band, who knew his secret…but now Alice was gone.

He'd made his decision to stay in the twenty-first century and only went back through the time gates for the festivals, some touring, and when the band was recording in the studio. But living near the time gate had unsettled him, so he had bought an island in the Caymans. Davy Morgan became a recluse and the press soon lost interest in him when they couldn't find him—or any scandal.

He cursed again, as his toe stubbed something large on the front porch. He took a step forward and tripped over a small bag. As he fell, he twisted to protect his guitar and landed on something soft; something that expelled a soft *oomph*.

"What the hell?" He grunted as his eyes adjusted to the faint light shining from the single lamp inside. He'd left it on after fumbling with the lock in the dark last night. It had taken half an hour to get the old key in the door. Living in an old country cottage was great for his privacy—most of the time—but it had its disadvantages. A night of singing at full volume had strained his vocal cords and all he wanted was a long, mellow whiskey to soothe his dry throat.

Dropping his gaze, he groaned as a pair of red-clad legs moved beneath him and he realised he was lying across a woman. A small, but *very* well-endowed woman. Wide eyes looked back at him above a white T-shirt stretched tight across her breasts.

"Well, you might as well come in. A good shag might just improve my night."

A soft gasp followed him as he put both hands on either side of her and pushed himself to his feet before retrieving his guitar from the ground.

"But you're not staying the night. Understood?" He looked around to the road. He hadn't noticed a vehicle parked in the dark laneway. "However, you got here, you can go back the same way."

Moving across to the door, he reached beneath the cushion of the padded chair next to the lintel and pulled out the huge key. The girl didn't speak as she pulled herself up from the ground.

"Come on. We'll be more comfortable inside." He opened the door and flicked the light switch as he waited for her to follow. When she stayed where she was, he turned and frowned as he noticed the luggage on his porch.

"No way, sweetheart. You're not staying. You've heard of 'wham, bam, thank you ma'am'? Well, if you want me in your pants, that's the deal. You get what you came for and then you leave. Okay?"

As he turned, the light fell on her face. Older than the usual groupie, she was tall, and dark shadows circled her large green eyes. Her hair was pulled back from her face and her mouth hung open.

"Well, are you coming in or not? Because I need a drink."

"Oh my God, you're Davy Morgan." Her voice was low and husky, and a ripple of something long forgotten ran down his back.

"David Morgan, at your service." He dipped in a sweeping bow before turning away from her. "And don't pretend you didn't know who I was when you came looking for me." Suspicion kicked in and he narrowed his eyes. "You didn't follow me back from the festival, did you?"

Of course she hadn't.

She'd been lying here on the porch when he'd come around the side. His biggest fear was someone following him and losing his privacy and his life here.

"How long have you been here?" he said tersely.

She continued to gape at him before she spoke. "But you can't be Davy Morgan. You're too young."

He gave a bitter laugh and pulled out his stock explanation. "Ah, you are obviously mistaking me for my uncle. The *famous* Davy Morgan? You're not familiar with me, the other David Morgan, then?"

"No. I'm not." Her eyes were riveted on him and they widened even more as she shook her head. "Why are you in my house?"

"*Your* house?" he said as he ran his hand through his hair. This one was obviously a nutcase. "Sorry, sweetheart, but good try. This is *my* house. Now, why don't you pick up your gear like a good little girl and go back to wherever you came from."

And he'd make sure she'd go and not come back. "Now I've had a look at you, you're too old for me and not my type. Great boobs but the haunted look doesn't do it for me." He tried to be as rude as he could. The sleazier he sounded, the quicker she'd get out of here and leave him in peace.

He stepped inside and pulled the door closed behind him and crossed to the makeshift bar on the old dresser. With a bit of luck, she'd take the hint and go before he had to think up any more coarse insults.

He ignored the pounding on the door as he uncapped the whiskey bottle.

"Oh, for fuck's sake." He muttered under his breath as he picked up his glass and walked back to the door. For the past forty years, he'd managed to avoid anyone discovering his secret. Having his

50

cottage as a bolt-hole had been a godsend. How had this girl found him?

He wrenched it open. "You can't be that desperate, darling?"

"You are a vile human being, whoever you are. Do the McLarens know you are squatting at their place?" Her voice conveyed her disgust and his interest was piqued as she stood on the porch, the light of battle in her eye. He glanced down at her chest. Her shoulders were back and she wasn't wearing a bra. Everything was on display, and to his disgust he felt a stirring of interest.

Hmm. A vile human being. That's exactly what he was.

"Ah…you're referring to the family of the late Alice McLaren, I guess?"

She nodded and spoke slowly, the wary look still in those shadowed eyes. "That would be correct."

He leaned against the lintel and sipped his whiskey. She held his gaze. Once you got past the purple shadows beneath her flashing eyes, and the rosy flush high on her cheekbones, she was really quite beautiful. Her lips were deep red and full, and her complexion was pale, despite the twin spots of colour signalling her anger. He hoped she'd stay angry. Women were trouble, and he was a sucker as soon as they went soft and pulled out the tears or quivering lips.

But not anymore. After having his privacy disturbed, she was lucky he was even having a conversation with her. He'd been manipulated in the past and he was not going to go there ever again, no matter how vulnerable the woman was.

"Well, sweetheart. If you weren't looking for me and a good shag—"

"Shag?" she interrupted. "Who says shag these days? You sound like Austin Powers." Her pretty lips tilted up in a brief smile.

"Who?" He shook his head and then set her straight. "I assume you're looking for Violet Cottage—which is next door." He inclined his head with a slight nod to the house next door.

"But the taxi dropped me here." Her shoulders sagged and it was like watching an exotic flower wilt beneath his gaze. Regret spiked in his chest for a brief moment, but he needed to be cruel to protect himself. Being alone was what he wanted.

"This is Rose Cottage. You'll find the key beneath—"

"I know where to look for the key. I just had the wrong cottage." She turned away and picked up a small bag and a laptop case. "Please accept my heartfelt apologies. I'm sorry your sexual thirst won't

52

be slaked tonight." The sarcasm dripped from her words and he smothered a grin. "You'll have to make do with your drink. I'll come back for my suitcase after I let myself into *Violet* Cottage."

Chapter Six

Megan found the key where Beth had said it would be. She turned it with trembling fingers and it unlocked the door with surprising ease. Exhaustion claimed her and as soon as she switched the light on, she headed for the first chair. Old fashioned floral fabrics and an overpowering smell of camphor filled the room and she slumped gratefully into the soft sofa.

She leaned her head back and groaned. The train had been late and when the taxi had finally dropped her at the cottage, she'd been unable to find the key where it was supposed to be. She'd pulled out her phone but it was dead and she couldn't charge it till she got inside, so she'd decided to camp out on the porch of the cottage until daylight and then head into the village to call Tony. From a distance, the muted sound of music reached her through the still air and her skin tingled with anticipation as she realised she was hearing the rehearsal from the festival.

And, of course, she'd ended up at the wrong bloody cottage. Why had things suddenly gone so wrong for her? Ever since her parents' accident, nothing in her life had seemed to go right.

She closed her eyes to rest...for a brief moment, and then she'd go back and get her suitcase. God, she was so tired. She'd gotten a lot of work done on the twenty-two-hour flight across from Australia but going more than twenty-four hours without sleep, and worrying about her appeal, had drained her. It had taken five hours to get out of terminal three at Heathrow and make her way across London to Paddington Station. She'd almost—only almost—been too tired to even appreciate being in *London*. A place she'd dreamed of visiting her whole life.

Then, at the almost-deserted railway station, it seemed as though she'd waited for hours for an old black cab to drive her down the never-ending country lanes until they had finally reached the cottage.

The wrong damn cottage.

Her face heated as she remembered the reception she'd gotten from the dark and brooding David Morgan.

When the light had first shone on his face and she'd seen those deep blue eyes staring at her, her heart had almost stopped beating. Davy Morgan was her idol and she knew his face intimately. In her teens, she'd scoured the retro shops and had found posters of him as well as David Bowie, Queen, and Bryan Ferry to cover her bedroom walls. While all her friends had been into nineties bands, she had loved listening to all the compilation CDs of seventies music and she'd uploaded them all to her iPod. She was sure she'd been born in the wrong time.

She grinned to herself. The posters of his uncle were still rolled up somewhere in a box along with her CDs of all his albums. She even had her parents' old vinyl records stowed away. In a special place—in her flat, and in her heart—was the record that Dad had bought for her on the day her parents had been killed.

Davy Morgan's songs had started her love affair with music. She hadn't even heard of this nephew, David Morgan, but if he was playing at Glastonbury, he must have some claim to fame. Probably cashing in on his uncle's reputation.

But he'd assumed she was a groupie, so he must have some fans of his own.

But what a jerk. Heat filled her cheeks as she recalled his words. A shag, for goodness' sake,

Wham, bam, thank you, ma'am. He wasn't even original. She knew her Bowie song lyrics, thank you very much.

56

And God, he was her neighbour. She hoped like hell he wasn't around when she went back to collect her bag. She'd just rest her eyes for a minute before she went back to get her bag, and *then* find a bed.

Alone in Violet Cottage.

The sun filtering through the narrow paned window and the twittering of an unfamiliar bird woke Megan. She lay on the soft sofa, pondering the birdsong, before the events of the previous day came crashing back. Closing her eyes, she groaned at the memory of last night and how she had ended up at the wrong house.

Megan cleared her mind, focusing on her breathing until her consciousness was directed inward. After a few moments, she was aware only of her inhaling and exhaling, until the tightness in her chest began to ease. Keeping her eyes closed, she let snatches of songs float through her mind. It was a technique she had perfected through her grief last year and she could now achieve it without any external aids.

No candles, no music. Just her own thoughts. Good thoughts.

She dozed again and woke a short time later, refreshed and calm. The sun was still shining in the window and the same bird was trilling away happily.

Wandering through the small cottage, she smiled at the contrast to her own apartment, which was always cluttered with books, papers, and music.

This little place was filled with knickknacks and crocheted doilies and dozens of framed photos. She climbed the narrow stairs and peeked into the two small bedrooms. The one facing the east was full of sunshine and she chose that one for her stay. Sitting on the bed, a wide grin broke across her face as she sank into the soft bedding, which was covered with a white candlewick bedspread.

She was in a cottage in the English countryside. It was all she could do not to break into a happy dance. Huge pink roses and trailing tendrils of green leaves papered the wall. She crossed the room to the window and looked across at the other cottage.

Rose Cottage was only a short distance away, across the emerald-green grass and a low fence. Too close for her peace of mind, but she'd just ignore the guy next door. Pushing the window open, she leaned out. The two small cottages were surrounded by open green fields with a narrow road lined with hedgerows winding away into the distance. On the horizon, the hill she knew from her research was Glastonbury Tor rose above the distant village. Church roofs and spires glinted in the bright sunlight and a sense of well-being stole over her as her problems receded. It was like coming home. In the field at the back of the cottages were three tall stone markers and Megan grinned. She wouldn't even have to take a tour to nearby Stonehenge now. It looked as though there were Neolithic monuments almost in the back garden.

Bright yellow roses tumbled over the fence between the two homes and in the distance, she could see the tents and stage being set up for the festival on the farm at Pilton. A frisson of anticipation ran through her and she smiled. She planned on heading over to have a look at the festival site as soon as she got settled, but first, she had to go next door and collect her suitcase. Hopefully, *he'd* gone out.

Going back down the steep wooden staircase to the ground floor of the cottage, she wandered into the kitchen. A huge ancient Aga stove filled the whole wall next to the door. She picked up the kettle and turned the tap at the old stone sink.

Nothing. Apart from a few creaks and groans and spits of rusty water. Opening the old refrigerator, she was pleased to see a jug of water and filled the kettle from that. It took a bit of fiddling to get the stove going but after a while she had a little gas flame alight. It would take a few minutes before the cold water in the kettle heated enough to have a coffee so she went into the small bathroom next to the kitchen to give her face a quick wash. But the tap there produced no water either. After running her fingers through her mussed hair, she straightened her now-crumpled T-shirt and jeans and went back into the kitchen. The whistling kettle was bubbling merrily on the stove and she switched the flame off and scrabbled through the cupboards for coffee.

Nothing. Not even a tea bag. Beth had said the cottage was rented out for the odd weekend, and she thought there might have been some coffee or tea bags, at least, in the cupboard. It looked like a walk into the village for some essentials was her first task for the day.

No, the second. First job was to collect her suitcase from next door and then, even if she couldn't wash, she could at least put on some clean clothes.

The sunshine was bright and warm at her back, although nowhere near as warm as summer in Sydney. Megan appreciated the fresh air and the sweet smell of the grass and the bluebells lining the path. Her heart beat a little faster as she walked slowly through the gate and along the footpath to the cottage next door, but there was no sign of life. The door was closed and all the windows were shut.

Great. He'd gone out or he was still in bed.

She quickly retrieved the suitcase and turned to go back to her cottage.

The door behind her creaked open and she put her head down and kept going, determined to ignore him.

"Morning, sweets." She stopped walking and turned around. The posh accent was at odds with the sight of the laid-back man leaning against the doorframe who lifted his cup and nodded at her.

Megan's breath caught in her throat and she stared at him unabashedly. Tight, low-slung black jeans were unbuttoned and his chest was bare. Her mouth dried as her gaze rose from his bare feet, up his legs, and skittered past the dark V of hair running into the top of his open jeans, and farther up to sleep-rumpled hair, with sexy dark stubble covering his strong jaw. He was a dead ringer for his uncle. He could have stepped straight from one of the posters that used to cover her walls.

"Cat got your tongue?"

Last night she hadn't noticed what a beautiful speaking voice he had. Deep and smooth with a melodious hint of a Welsh accent, but the hard line of his jaw and his closed expression didn't quite fit with the sexy voice. She held his gaze and drew a quick breath. Dark-blue eyes surrounded by long dark eyelashes stared back at her. His unsmiling gaze was fixed on her face but she still self-consciously tugged her crumpled T-shirt down over her bare midriff without speaking.

"Ah, she has lost her voice." He said to no one in particular before tipping the mug to his mouth and taking a sip. The smell of freshly brewed coffee drifted across and Megan's nose twitched. She put her suitcase down and pulled herself up straight, meeting his gaze.

"No, I haven't lost my voice," she said. "I was wondering if I could speak to you without getting another crude proposition."

He laughed. "Up to you, sweetheart. But it wouldn't be a bad way to start the day, if you are interested. Guaranteed to get the blood pumping."

His gaze pinned her and as his lips tipped up, she realised he was teasing.

She knew she needed to lighten up. Her life for the past few months had made her way too serious.

"I came for my suitcase, but I wouldn't say no to one of those." She looked at the coffee cup in his hand. "I haven't had time to shop, and I thought there might be something in the cottage, but there's not even a stray tea bag."

"Not surprised. No one's been there all summer," he said. His intent gaze stayed on her face and Megan's neck prickled. There was something about this man that unsettled her. She'd come across arrogant musicians like him as she'd interviewed them for her research, but his resemblance to his uncle unnerved her.

"I suppose I can stretch to some coffee." He stepped through the door and she stepped forward, about to follow him into his home, but he stopped her with a curt command over his shoulder. "Wait there."

Megan did as she was told, stayed on the porch and looked out over the green fields. If he didn't want her inside, that was fine by her. The less she had to do with the rude musician, the better for her peace of mind.

And God knows she needed peace, and nothing more to stress her.

The air was still and the sound of the bees buzzing in the roses in the cottage garden drifted across to her. A couple of minutes later, David appeared at the door with a different mug in his hand and passed it to her.

"Cream and sugar. You could do with fattening up."

Maybe, just maybe, there was a kind person beneath that aggressive exterior. He'd brought her coffee and in Megan's books that was one way to get in her good graces. Undeniably, there were good looks and a kind of charm…or rather a dangerous attraction. He stepped back inside and turned to her. "Keep the cup. Consider it a welcome gift."

The door shut in her face and all was quiet, apart from the bees and the occasional mooing of a cow.

Okay, take back the thoughts of him being kind or having basic manners.

No. No charm at all. The less I see of him, the better. Bemused, she shook her head and took a sip of the hot coffee before grabbing the handle of the suitcase and dragging it along the path back to her cottage.

Chapter Seven

David was tired and still in a filthy mood. The last thing he'd wanted to see was the Aussie woman on his doorstep again. The last two days had been a total loss as far as rehearsals went. First, the electrical setup had failed and then the stage had collapsed and they'd had to pull the pin on a full rehearsal for the second day in a row. He was worried that they were going to look like fools at the concert on Saturday night. They were opening for Bowie and the crowd was predicted to be huge for this second festival.

Then Holly had presented him with that bloody newspaper. She'd jumped around in excitement, telling him what great media coverage it was, and how she couldn't have set up anything better if she'd tried.

"It'll pull the crowds in, Davy." Her face was lit up in a grin beneath that stupid red hat she thought made her look like a hippie. "They so love a bad boy."

Bear had glanced over at him and had shaken his head slightly, as if to say "don't lose your cool," but David had lost it anyway. Holly had opened her mouth to speak but he'd wrenched the paper from her hands and torn it in half.

"Get rid of it, and don't encourage them. The only publicity I want is about how good our music is. None of that other gossip shite. Is that clear?" He'd glared at her and wasn't aware he'd taken her arm until Slim came over and pulled her away from him. David dropped the torn pages onto the floor and kicked at them. "For Christ's sake. They write lies, and all you can say is that it will pull the fucking crowds in?"

Holly had scurried away across the stage. "You want to sell records, Davy? You put up with it." She'd looked at him defiantly as she stood at a safe distance, behind Bear and his drums. "Get over it. And all publicity *is* good. You want to make the big time or not?"

"I don't care what they make up. It has nothing to do with our music."

"Ah, a purist." Holly's voice was cynical. "You want truth and light, man. Maybe you'd better go and join a symphony orchestra and play classical music for the BBC."

David shook his head and forgot all about Holly and her drivel as he moved across to the kitchen window to tip his coffee dregs into the sink. A movement next door caught his attention. His new neighbour was wandering around in her back garden. He'd dreamed about her all night. He'd been so wired, that he'd gotten up early to do some writing. Rose-red lips, glorious hair, and a body begging to be loved; it was as if she'd bewitched him. The crazy dreams had stayed with him after he had woken up, dreams of touching her and his hands overflowing with her tears even as he held her breasts. She'd stared deep into his eyes and he'd felt as though his soul had been exposed to her. He'd still been thinking about her when she appeared on his porch this morning.

But she'd come back over to get her bag, not to connect with him. He'd forgotten all about it, or he would have put it on her porch last night. He'd gotten a jolt in his chest when he'd heard her out there. Despite the crumpled shirt and jeans, she looked like something out of a fairy-tale. All that tumbling hair and those bright-red lips.

And she had attitude.

It was a shame he wasn't interested. He frowned and shook his head.

I'm not.

After he'd strummed his guitar softly in the early hours, new words and notes had poured out of him and he'd written a great new song. The only reason he was unsettled was because of the rehearsal fiasco, nothing to do with his next-door neighbour. He was always on edge before a concert.

But to stay safe, he'd ignore her presence next door. His cottage had been private for the past few years; the one she was in wasn't rented very often and the owners never came near it.

The phone rang and pulled him out of his thoughts.

Clive, his banker, greeted him and he moved back to the window and watched the girl as she stood in the backyard. She stared out across the fields, sipping from the mug he had handed her. He realised he didn't even know her name, but damn it, he was intrigued. It was the dreams that were getting him wound up, not her.

"David, are you listening to me?"

"Yeah, I'm listening."

"You're going to have to come to the city today and sign some papers."

"I can't. Rehearsal got messed up yesterday. I can't come to London until after the festival."

He leaned his head on the window and rubbed the back of his neck with his free hand.

Why was life always so bloody complicated?

"If you can't come to London, I'll meet you halfway. Or better still, I can try to get the documents expressed to a bank down where you are."

"Send them to Taunton. I'll drive across first thing in the morning. What's so hell-fired urgent, Clive?"

"The latest transfer to the Caymans. There's a new condition you have to initial before we can transfer the funds. I can't do it for you."

David sighed. "All right. If you can't get it there by tomorrow, make sure you let me know. I don't want to make a trip for nothing. We're bloody short of time."

"Yes, and I know what a perfectionist you are." Clive ended the call and David glanced out the window again, but she was gone. It was time to head across to the farm for rehearsal. He'd spent more than enough time mooning around like a lovesick teenager.

Five minutes later, David had thrown on a T-shirt and grabbed his guitar. He opened the back gate, ignoring the woman who was now sitting in an alcove at the back of the cottage next door.

Shit. One of the reasons he stayed in this place for the festival was because it was so isolated. He could come and go as he pleased without being seen.

If she made a habit of sitting there, he was going to have to be very careful.

Taking a different path than usual, he crossed the newly mown grass and walked along the path to the River Brue, before doubling back to the intersection of the ley lines to find the gate. The houses were in the distance and he raised one hand to shade his eyes and see if she was watching, but there was no sign of her. Finding the stone markers, he stepped to the line and closed his eyes as the air shimmered around him.

***

Megan had tried to call Tony as soon as she woke up, before it was too late at night back home in Australia, but her phone had gone dead. She'd tried to charge it but she'd forgotten all about the different power outlets here. Hopefully, it wasn't too far to the village because she'd need to buy an adapter. While she was there, she would try to find a computer to check her e-mail because her laptop didn't work either.

After she placed her suitcase inside the front door, she wandered out back with her coffee and found a lovely little nook covered in a vine with pretty pink flowers spilling along the back of the cottage. A small table and chairs were tucked into the sunny corner. She looked around with surprise. For a house that no one lived in, the garden was neat and tidy and the grass was clipped. The roses along the fence needed deadheading, but apart from that, the backyard was pretty.

With a quick brush of the dead leaves off the table, she settled down to a lovely view of the grassy fields. The fragrance of the roses and violets overlaid the aroma of the coffee and she closed her eyes and took a deep breath. Truly a beautiful place.

Soothing for my soul.

It was much needed and she was so grateful to Beth's family for letting her stay here for the duration of her visit. And even the Davy Morgan look-alike next door had shown some manners this morning.

Until he slammed the door in my face.

She tipped her head back to the bright morning sun. Nothing seemed as bad as it had last night. A good night's sleep, despite being filled with bizarre dreams about a rock star with long black curls and deep blue eyes, had left her refreshed and with a strange warmth low in her belly. As she sat out in the fresh clean air, serenity stole over her. The sound of a lone tractor winding up and down around the field between her and the village was the only sound, apart from the birds. Glancing at her watch, she was taken aback to see it was almost noon. She was going to have to walk into Glastonbury to get the power

71

adapter and some food and find a plumber to sort this lack of water out. Leaning forward, she emptied the now cold coffee into the garden as a movement at the back of the cottage next door caught her attention. A tall dark figure slipped through the fence and walked across the field, with a guitar slung casually over his shoulder. The sun glinted off his jet-black hair and he glanced across but didn't even acknowledge her with a wave.

Megan looked away and ignored him, and by the time she glanced back through the kitchen window as she put the mug in the sink, he had disappeared.

Fine. He'd kindly given her coffee but she'd ignore him from now on. If he wanted to be as rude and obnoxious as he'd been last night, she wanted nothing more to do with him. She might see him playing at the festival. As soon as she got to a computer, she'd Google him. As far as she knew, she'd never seen a mention of him in the line-up of bands. She knew her music inside out, but she'd never heard of Davy Morgan having a nephew who was well known enough to play at Glastonbury. And as far as she knew, *her* Davy Morgan, the idol of her teenage years, was still alive and had retired to the Cayman Islands.

##

"Sorry, love. No Wi-Fi, no phone, and cell service is spotty." The grooves on either side of the woman's mouth deepened as she frowned. "The magnetics have been on the rise more than usual this year. It's the summer solstice coming on."

Megan shook her head, not having a clue of what the crazy woman in the village shop was talking about. Clad in a bright-purple apron and bright-green leggings, with her steel-grey hair scraped back into a severe bun, she had been talking nonstop since Megan stepped into the dingy shop. All she wanted to do was call or e-mail Beth and Tony, and let them know she was settled in the cottage and to find out any more news about her suspension.

"What do you mean, the magnetics?"

The woman shook her arms and a jangle of coloured plastic bracelets clattered together on her wrists.

"The lines? Ye've not heard of the lines?" She leaned her arms on the counter of the dark, cluttered store.

Megan shook her head again. "No."

"The ley lines are the connections between the ancient monuments." She looked at Megan as though she was the crazy one. "When the summer and winter solstices arrive each year, they play havoc with everything. Phone, Internet, water."

The shopkeeper wrapped up the packet of coffee, the bottle of milk, and the fruit Megan had brought to the counter. She placed it all in a brown paper bag along with the can of soup Megan had chosen for her dinner.

"Do you sell power adapters here?"

"No, love. You'll have to go into Taunton for that." The woman looked curiously at her as she passed her the groceries. "Just here for the festival, are you?" she asked.

"Yes, I am." Megan handed over some money.

"Are you staying in the pub or camping out at the farm?"

"I'm staying at the McLaren cottage."

The woman passed the package across the counter. "Say hello to Alice for me if you see her."

"Alice?" Megan stared at her in confusion. "I thought she'd passed away?"

The woman nodded. "Yes, two winters back. But she loved her little cottage and she's been seen there a few times since then."

Megan gripped the bag of groceries and headed through the dim shop towards the door. It looked as though she wasn't going to get a sensible conversation in here, but the woman kept talking as she came from behind the counter and followed Megan to the door.

"Well, you watch yourself getting to the festival. Make sure you take the road. Don't go crossing those fields. There are mounds and marker stones scattered all the way from Alice's cottage to the Pilton farm." She followed Megan past the crowded shelves. "If you're not careful, dear, you're likely to find yourself who knows when. A lot of people have gone missing at this time of the year. God knows where they've ended up."

The woman walked across to the shelf, shaking her head and muttering, as Megan headed for the door, and sunshine, and sanity.

Haunted cottages and ending up in another time? Was the woman demented?

Surely there was a post office in this little village. Or maybe the pub had a Wi-Fi connection?

"Oh, and dear?" The querulous old voice followed her to the door and she paused.

"How's your water?"

"My water?"

What the heck is she talking about?

"Is the water still working in Alice's cottage?"

"Ah, no. There's something wrong with the pipes."

"Don't worry. It'll come back on after the solstice. It's all the witching rods they're using down at the festival looking for the springs. In the meantime,

75

you'd better buy up on the bottled water." The woman bustled back around the counter and reached beneath and followed Megan outside. "Here's a couple of bottles to keep you going. I'll get Ned to drop a water container off when he comes back from his deliveries, so you can bathe."

Megan reached into her purse but the woman shook her head

"No worries. If you are staying in Alice's cottage, I'll add it to the account and you can settle up when you go. Now you take good care, dear, and heed my words. I heard they found the spring at the farm for this newfangled stage and everyone on the southern line lost their water."

Megan forced a smile onto her face as she backed out of the store. "Thank you, I will." She couldn't get out of there quick enough.

Crazy woman.

She'd go find some lunch and ask where she could find a plumber to sort out the water problem.

There was no sign of a post office, but a whitewashed pub was located on the other side of the village green. Megan wanted to pinch herself. This quaint English village was just as she'd imagined it would be. A couple of white geese wandered across the street, honking as they headed to the small brook running behind the shops. She pushed open the door of the old tavern building and was relieved to see it full of young people in casual clothes. After ordering her lunch, she picked up a drink from the bar and headed out the back towards the last vacant table. There was no sign of a computer or even a public phone, and thoughts of her appeal began to crowd into her head as the worry of not being able to contact home tugged at her.

She put her head back and closed her eyes, ignoring the sick feeling in her stomach. Taking a deep breath, she focused on the warmth of the sun on her skin, letting her mind drift to that place deep inside where she could ignore the problems waiting for her at home.

Focus on the present. Deep breathing.

The warmth on her shoulders suddenly increased, and she opened her eyes to a pair of deep blue eyes staring down at her.

Turning her groan into a cough, she stared back at him.

"Well?" David said. The look on her neighbour's face indicated he expected some sort of an answer. She shrugged her shoulder and pushed away his hand but the pleasant warmth lingered even after his hands were back by his side.

"Well, what?" she asked primly.

"Can we share your table?"

Megan glanced behind him. Two other men who were engaged in a heated conversation were obviously the 'we' he referred to.

"It's a big table for one person and the pub is packed. Unless you're expecting company?"

She moved down on the bench and shook her head. "No, go ahead. I'm just having a quick lunch and then you can have the table to yourselves."

"Don't rush on our account, love." The big man standing behind David slid onto the bench opposite her and held a beefy hand out. "Davy said you're his new neighbour, so we didn't think you'd mind us asking to share your table. Any friend of Davy is a friend of the band's."

Megan reached over and took the proffered hand as the guy kept talking. "I'm Bear and this is Slim. We play backup for Davy, here. Stage isn't ready so we came to grab a bite before we start rehearsal this afternoon." A tall guy with shoulder-length hair in a black T-shirt gave her a wave from the other end of the table. A frisson of familiarity ran through her.

Bear and Slim? She knew those names from somewhere. She racked her brain but couldn't remember where. Maybe their names were on the program she'd read for the festival?

Holding her breath, she glanced to the side as her neighbour from next door slid onto the bench beside

78

her. He looked at her without smiling and her breath caught. The uncanny resemblance to his uncle was striking and she felt like a star-struck teenager with her mouth gaping open.

"All settled in?"

"Almost." She turned away from him and tried to gather her composure. "I just need to get the water turned on and find a Wi-Fi connection."

Bear threw his head back and laughed. "Good luck, sweets. Everything's haywire here at the moment."

David frowned at him and interjected. "Yes, a cable must have been cut when they were setting up the festival. Wi-Fi seems to be down all around the district."

She looked at him curiously. "Do you live here all the time or are you on holiday?"

"I live here some of the time. Why?"

"I was wondering if you could recommend a plumber. There seems to be no water at the cottage."

"No, I couldn't." His voice was terse and he obviously didn't want to talk to her. Megan moved her leg away, trying to ignore the warmth of his jean-clad thigh close to hers.

Moody bastard. She'd shared her table on his request. If he couldn't be civil, he could go find another table.

While he stared away in the distance, the other two men engaged her in conversation for a few minutes. To her relief, all of their meals arrived at the same time.

She wouldn't have to stay and be polite too long. The last thing she felt like was being sociable in a pub; even if it was an English pub and a beautiful afternoon.

"So you're here for the festival?" Bear looked at her across his bowl of chips and she was aware of David pausing as she answered.

"Yes, I'm here to do some research for my thesis," she replied.

"We can get you some backstage passes if you want." Bear winked at her and took a swig of his second pint of beer.

"No, thank you. Mr. Morgan here has already made me a few offers, which I've rejected."

Bear slapped his thigh and his booming laugh sounded around the garden, and a few heads turned. "Was he rude to you? He tries to keep this bad-boy rock star thing going."

Megan looked at David to gauge his mood but his expression was inscrutable. "Let's just say, I know that David doesn't like having neighbours."

"Well, that's because—"

"Bear." David's voice was clipped and the other man stopped talking immediately. "Put a lid on it. You've had too much beer in the sun."

After a moment, Bear dropped his eyes and muttered into his drink. "Sorry. Forgot when we were."

"*Where* we were," David said loudly.

"Yeah, where we were."

Megan gathered up the paper her sandwich had been wrapped in and stood. "I'll leave you to it. It was nice to meet you."

Actually, it was decidedly unpleasant; the friendly conversation had ceased and the atmosphere had become uncomfortable, but they could still help her out with a bit of local knowledge.

"Do you know where I would find a phone that works or an Internet connection that hasn't been affected by the cut cable?"

She was surprised to notice a furtive glance between the two men, who both turned to David.

"You really need to get access?" His voice was reluctant.

"I need to check my e-mail and call home. My cell is dead and I need to buy a power adapter." She expelled her breath and continued. "It's not life-threatening, but I do really need to check on a situation that I left at home before I left Australia."

81

"Man trouble?" David stood and shook the crumbs from his shirt.

"No, I don't have 'man' trouble." Her voice was terse.

For goodness' sake, was the man focused on sex?

"I have an issue at work to sort out." Megan gathered up her grocery parcels and turned to him before she walked away. She lifted her chin and stared at him. "Luckily it's only men who base everything on sex or the world would be in chaos."

Bear and Slim burst out laughing and she nodded at them.

"Nice to meet you, gentlemen. I might see you on stage."

They grinned and Bear shook his head.

"Not this year," he said enigmatically.

As she walked around the corner of the pub back towards the green, a hand grabbed at her arm and she came to a sudden stop. Slowly turning around, she looked into a black T-shirt and raised her eyes to meet the deep blue gaze fixed on her. She waited as David stared at her.

He ran his other hand through his loose black curls and a shiver trickled down her back, contrasting with the warmth of his hand still gripping the top of her arm. Their gazes met and held, and the feeling intensified. Her blood hummed in response to his look and she swallowed, waiting for him to speak.

"Look, I'm sorry for being so rude last night." His voice was deep. "I thought you knew who I was and that you'd come looking for me." His mouth lifted slightly in a wry grin. "It sounds egotistical, but as strange as you might find it, it does happen, you know."

"Well, you needn't worry about me because I've never heard of you." Megan still hadn't forgotten the assumptions he'd made last night. She kept her voice cold as she fought the warmth rushing through her body. David still held her arm firmly, and the heat radiated from his fingers and ended up low in her belly.

"That's good." He ran his other hand through his loose curls. "Look, all I want is privacy. This time of the year with the festival brings all types of people into town. We've had a few journalists in the village trying to dig up some dirt on us. Anything to sell a magazine or newspaper." He looked away and seemed to be talking to himself. "They never seem to let the truth get in the way of a good story."

"I know what you mean." But despite feeling a measure of sympathy, she looked pointedly down at his hand. He didn't take the hint and Megan fought the desire to lean into his chest. His words had resonated with her and she clenched her fists. He was so close to her, his woodsy cologne enveloped her and she stepped back, catching her breath.

"Look, I can probably help you and be a bit neighbourly. I have to go into Taunton tomorrow morning, so if you want to come with me, the offer is there. There's are a few cafés and a library with Wi-Fi. There's nothing in the village. We're a bit behind the times here."

For a moment, Megan considered refusing his offer and then realised she couldn't afford to. She had to see what was happening back in Sydney. How Tony was progressing with the appeal. And also checking that Kathy was okay.

And whether I'll have a job to go back to. She could buy a power adapter while they were there, and then she could charge her cell phone and her laptop and not have to depend on him being neighbourly. She sensed he was already regretting the offer to help her out. David Morgan was a strange man.

"Thank you. That's very kind."

"Be ready at eight. I'm only going in for an hour or so. I have to be back for rehearsal. With all the problems we've had, we're way behind."

He turned on his heel and headed back to his band members, but not before Megan noticed how well his jeans fit a set of powerful thighs.

She reached up and brushed her fingers across the top of her arm where he had gently gripped her.

Get over it. That's the last thing I need. A holiday fling.

Just use him as an opportunity to find out more about Davy Morgan. What an opportunity had landed in her lap. Meeting the nephew of the man she'd been obsessed with since her teens.

What were the chances of that? She'd be crazy to let it go.

A smile tugged at her lips. As crazy as the woman in the grocery store.

If nothing else, her first twenty-four hours in England had been far from boring.

Chapter Eight

Vivid dreams plagued Megan's sleep and she sat up in bed, her breath coming in short gasps. It was pitch dark and she was wide awake. Images of bare-chested sweaty rock stars with black curly hair, on stage in tight leather pants and belting out loud music, had woken her and she'd lain there with her eyes open for a moment before she sat up, and then she realised that real music was actually pounding through the darkness from the house next door.

She'd thumped her pillow and put her head beneath the blankets but now her mind turned to worry about the appeal. Being out of contact was absolutely frustrating and she lay there wondering whether she should go home a bit earlier than she'd originally planned. Was there even any point in continuing her research? Control of her life seemed to be slipping through her fingers.

Chances were there'd be no job to go back to, anyway. Maybe she could spend the rest of her life in this pretty cottage. Not such a bad alternative.

The music drifted in from next door and Megan closed her eyes as Davy Morgan's voice came across to her in the still of the night. She closed her eyes and let the music wash over her. Tears rolled down her cheeks. It was one of his sad love songs that she'd always loved.

"I'll love you wherever you are, whenever you are."

The ability of music to change moods and to promote well-being in its listeners had fascinated her since she'd first listened to those Davy Morgan songs in her teens, and that had been the catalyst for her study of music. Now it was flowing through her like a drug and she embraced the high. She had to put the fiasco at home out of her mind and make the most of being here at Glastonbury. The opportunity to enrich her sociology of music thesis was something she needed to embrace. Her throat closed as the music swelled to a crescendo and she drew a deep breath as euphoria flooded through her.

No matter what was happening at home, and what went down with her job at the university, she was here because of her love for the music and the innate desire to find out more about the seventies and the festivals. If it didn't end up contributing to her doctorate, did it really matter? The knowledge and the music filled an empty place within her soul.

Music had the ability to take over her soul and fill her with love. It completed her, and made everything seem worthwhile.

Suddenly, the music stopped before reaching the final riff, and she felt cheated. But when it went back to the beginning and started again, Megan smiled.

Just the same as she'd played that song over and over when she was a teenager.

She lay back and waited for it to get to the end again, but it chopped off before the final rise. By the time he had played the song and stopped it eight or more times, frustration filled her.

No wonder David Morgan didn't want neighbours if he was going to play his uncle's music at full volume. The song stopped and started jerkily; sometimes halfway through lines, before going back to the beginning of the song. It went on for an hour or more. After another ten stops and starts, Megan put the pillow over her head and burrowed into the soft mattress.

Why the hell was he playing it like that?

She couldn't stand it. He was ruining the music she loved.

##

The next thing Megan knew there was pounding on the door downstairs and she opened her eyes to bright sunshine.

She'd overslept. Jumping out of bed, she grabbed a loose T-shirt and threw it on and pulled it down over her legs before running down the stairs and opening the door. She peered through the narrow opening as her fingers clutched the door.

David was leaning against the post on the small porch.

"So, I was just checking. You've changed your mind about coming to Taunton?" He didn't smile and she got the impression he was hoping she'd agree with his assumption.

"No, I slept in." She glared at him. "You playing your uncle's music at full volume kept me awake most of the night."

That got a strange look out of him, before he glanced at his watch. "So how long till you can be ready?"

"Five minutes. I've still got no water for a shower, so I'll just get dressed. I can grab a coffee in...where are we going?"

"Taunton."

The water delivery promised by the crazy purple-clad lady in the village store hadn't arrived, so Megan made do with a quick wash with a flick of water out of the last of her drinking water. She was in dire need of a shower and a hair wash after the long flight and twenty-four hours in the cottage. She pulled her hair up and wound it into a knot on the back of her head before slipping on a clean pair of jeans and a loose cotton shirt. A good spray of perfume and she flew down the stairs. At least clean clothes made her feel a bit more respectable.

"Are you sure you don't know any plumbers?"

David shook his head as he opened the door of an old sporty vehicle of some type. It looked like one of those cars in the Austin Powers movies she loved. It was a bright-red convertible and the top was down.

"Never needed one in my cottage. Sorry," he said.

"Wow, I feel like I'm back in the sixties," she exclaimed. "What is this?"

"1966 Austin Healey 3000."

"Is this like the one out of that Austin Powers movie?"

"No that was an E-Type Jaguar…the *Shaguar*…remember?" He looked across and for the first time a glimmer of a smile crossed his face. "You probably think that's more suitable for a rock star?"

"Are you a rock star, David?" She looked at him curiously. "I don't mean to be rude, but I've never heard of you. What's your band called?"

The resemblance to his uncle was amazing. Every time she glanced across at him, she wanted to giggle like a silly teenager. It would be interesting to hear him perform at the festival. From what he had been playing last night, it seemed like he did covers of his uncle's songs.

As soon as they got back from town she was going to walk across the fields and listen to the rehearsal. She'd made sure she'd gotten a ticket that gave her access to the farm before the festival kicked off. No matter what the crazy hippie shopkeeper had said about magnetics and ley lines. Megan shook her head; she felt like she'd stumbled into an alternative world. It would be a great opportunity to interview singers and roadies before the festival proper began.

David put the car into gear and roared up the narrow road without answering her question about his band. Megan grabbed for her hair as the wind caught it and it flew around her face.

"So do you want me to find you a plumber?" he asked, changing the subject.

"If you could, that would be great."

"First off, I'll come over and have a look when we get back." His brow furrowed. "Look, I don't want to rush you but we can only stay an hour or so in Taunton. I'll drop you off at a café and you can get your caffeine hit and check your e-mail at the same time."

"That'll be long enough. I just need to see what's happening at home." She let out her breath in a sigh and he looked across at her.

"Problems?" he said.

"A problem at work. If it's not sorted, I'll have no job to go back to."

"What do you do?"

He actually sounded interested so she gave him the short version of her career. He didn't need to know all the details. "I do some lecturing and tutoring in the sociology of music while I'm working on my PhD. It was actually your Uncle Davy who fostered my love of seventies music."

He glanced across at her as he changed a gear and the car took off down a narrow hill. "Hmm. Interesting."

All was quiet until they drove into a medium-sized town and David dropped her off on the main street.

"There's a café that should have computers about halfway along. I'll pick you up here in an hour. Okay?" he asked.

"What about an electrical store? I need an adapter."

He pointed one out across from the café. Megan grabbed her bag and climbed out of the car, taking note of the cafe name so she didn't get lost.

***

It only took five minutes for David to meet with the bank manager and sign the transfer for it to be couriered back to Clive at his bank in London. The royalties from his music were still providing him with a luxurious lifestyle in the twenty-first century and enabled him to split his time between Glastonbury and his island in the Bahamas.

He wandered along the main street, which was lined with a mixture of old buildings from previous centuries and modern glass-and-concrete structures. Glancing at his watch, he turned into the courtyard of the Castle Hotel, where he knew he could get a quick coffee in the BRAZZ brasserie beneath the imposing four-story structure.

He loved the old castle, and he'd stayed there a few times before he'd bought the cottage. An ancient wisteria vine with a trunk as thick as a tree rose from the walls beside the entrance and covered them with soft purple blooms. Once a Norman fortress and reconstructed in the eighteenth century, the Castle at Taunton had been welcoming travellers since the twelfth century and David idly wondered how hard it would be to find a time gate to go back and see it in its heyday.

Too risky. Alice had constantly warned him about using the ley line gates just to satisfy his curiosity about the past.

He shook his head as he sipped his coffee and pondered the problem of Megan. He'd finally found out her name before they'd started the short trip to

Taunton. He'd tried to avoid her at the pub yesterday, but Bear had pushed him on. Life was complicated enough without having her next door and seeing him head for the stones every day. When she arrived at this year's festival and he and the band weren't playing, she was going to be asking some difficult questions.

He'd have to spin her some story about their act being canned from the current line-up to explain their nonappearance this year. But more importantly, he'd have to keep Megan away from the stones.

He could still smell her perfume from being in the car with her, despite the top being down. She must have plastered it on but he'd been relieved when her hair had been pulled back and she'd looked less like the woman he'd been dreaming about for the past two nights.

Bloody hell, I don't need this complication.

Pushing back his chair, he stood and gestured to the bar attendant, pointing to the money he'd left on the table. The pretty girl gave him a wave and held his eye, but he had no reaction to her come-hither look. His head was full of the red-haired beauty from next door. His dreams about her had left him curiously content, but restless, and he couldn't shake the feeling that he was going to have to do something about it.

There was an inevitability about it that he was trying to deny.

Megan was waiting for him at the intersection as he'd asked. She'd wound her hair up and secured it with some sort of clip.

"Thanks for being on time," he said as she slipped in and closed the door. Huge sunglasses covered her eyes and her lips were tight. He risked a quick glance across at her and frowned as she brushed the back of her hand across her cheek.

"You okay?" Not that he really needed to know, but sympathy settled in his gut as she drew a shaky breath and then tried to disguise it with a cough.

"Fine." She didn't speak again as they travelled through the outskirts of the small town. A couple of times, she brushed her hand to her eyes but said nothing.

David shrugged and focused on his driving. The small sports car ate up the miles quickly and it was less than half an hour when he turned onto the narrow unpaved lane that led down to the two cottages. As soon as he stopped the car outside her place, Megan opened the door and grabbed her bag.

"Thanks for the lift. Appreciate it." She flicked him a quick wave as she shut the door and headed off down the path towards the front door of Violet Cottage. David put the car into gear and drove the short distance to the small barn on the other side of Rose Cottage.

***

Megan pulled the clip from her hair and shook her hair loose before wandering through the kitchen. Casually picking up an apple from the shopping bag she'd left on the counter yesterday, and grateful for the large coffee she'd had in town, she stepped out the back door. She was still gob smacked by the e-mail from Tony. Her chest closed and she fought the rising panic as she slipped through the back door.

Documentary evidence of e-mails and finances supplied by VC was in the subject line of the email. Tony's e-mail had been brief.

Attached. Megan WTF is going on?

He'd attached an audit and she'd managed to print that, and the e-mail, fold them and shove them into her pocket. The late-morning sun was still bathing the patio in sunshine and she slid onto a chair and put her head down on her crossed arms as weariness overwhelmed her. The same lethargy she'd experienced when her parents had been killed overtook her limbs and Megan blinked as her vision blurred.

Jet lag and interrupted sleep last night. That's all it was.

She was not going to let herself sink into a depression just because some lowlife at the university had accessed her computer files. That had to be what had happened. There was no other explanation. She got a sense from the tone of Tony's e-mail that he was beginning to doubt her innocence too. Her own brother-in-law was sceptical, so what chance did she have of proving she hadn't done any of the things she'd been accused of? Looked more and more likely that someone had gone to great lengths to get her out of the department. Out of her job, and out of the university.

It had to be Greg; she had underestimated him and she hadn't given him credit for his determination to get her out of her job.

He was a nut case; it hadn't taken her long to figure that out. She'd seen the crazy side of him and had broken off their short relationship when she'd overheard him in a call to an ex-girlfriend one night. He was abusive and cruel, and she'd not been out with him again.

Squeezing her eyes shut, she pressed her fingers to her temples, trying to remember if Greg had ever had access to her password. They'd gone out for a few months and he'd suckered her right in. All he'd been after was the full-time lecturer's position and any information that she had on the selection panel. He'd trampled all over her in the race for promotion. And he'd worked hard to get in her bed, wining her and dining her, and taking her away for romantic weekends. She'd fallen for it hook, line and sinker, needing the comfort and attention in the months after the accident.

She had sworn off men for life when she'd realised what he was doing. He'd actually had the temerity to brag to his ex about it when he'd thought Megan wasn't listening. She'd told him to leave her apartment and demanded the key back from him. Now, she realised, he'd obviously been in her files in her home office.

She'd never given him her password but he'd obviously figured it out somehow. She'd make him pay, if it was the last thing she did.

But no more of this mooning around. She'd go to the festival rehearsal, get some more food from the crazy lady at the village store, and chase up a plumber. And then when she got home, she'd figure out a plan of attack. She was going to fight to keep her job.

Sitting up straight, she squinted into the bright sunlight as the creak of a gate caught her attention. David was heading out the back of his cottage across the fields, his guitar slung over his shoulder, and he was obviously going to rehearse at the festival at

Pilton. If she didn't hurry, she'd miss the afternoon rehearsals. No more sitting around feeling sorry for herself. She'd grab her notebook and camera, go start her research, and enjoy herself while she was there too.

##

First stop was the village, and she walked along the road rather than cutting across the fields. The main street was quiet and she headed for the pub—there'd be more chance of getting local information there. The hippie woman in the shop had been less than helpful yesterday.

"Wait!" A shrill voice came from behind and Megan turned around. The purple apron was flapping in front of the plump shopkeeper who was wearing orange tights today. Megan smothered a grin.

"Sorry, love. Just wanted to tell you, Ned is dropping your water off at the cottage later." The woman huffed as she came to a stop beside Megan. "He got in late last night and I forgot to tell him to deliver it to you. He had a long cab fare to London."

"No problem. I'm just…er…going to the pub to see if they can find me a plumber."

"No, no, no." The woman shook her head and her long earrings jangled as her head moved. "No point, love. Another twenty-four hours to the solstice and whoosh…before you know it, everything will be

99

working again as good as gold." She reached over and gave Megan a motherly pat on the cheek. "You'll see."

Megan shrugged and headed off down the road, looking at the festival map that had been delivered along with her ticket.

Damn…I've gone the wrong way.

She'd totally lost her sense of direction—being in the Northern Hemisphere had thrown her and she had to think before she got her bearings. Pilton was actually closer to Shepton Mallet and it would have been quicker to go across the fields from her place than walk into Glastonbury and go around. It was only a two-mile walk that way. By coming into the village, she'd added about six miles to her trip if she wanted to continue on to the farm where the festival was. She flipped over the map and looked at the bus schedule, but the buses didn't start running from the village until the festival proper kicked off tomorrow.

With a sigh, she turned back to the shop to collect supplies for a decent meal tonight. This afternoon she'd charge her phone and focus on the e-mail from Tony and then make sure she was up bright and early tomorrow to go to the festival.

***

For the first time, everything had gone according to plan on stage. Holly hadn't shown up, and David was pleased with the rehearsal. Just as he crossed the field and lined up the markers, the sun set in a blaze of colour that highlighted Saint Michael's Tower on the top of Glastonbury Tor. The air softened immediately. He loved the long English dusk and he missed it when he was on his Caribbean island.

The only thing that had stuffed up rehearsal today was worrying about Megan. For the life of him, he couldn't understand why the woman stayed in his thoughts. He didn't like what was happening to him. He'd dreamed about her and she was fixed in his mind. Perhaps it was the solstice that was screwing with his head.

Yeah, she loved his songs, and yeah, she was a looker, but she'd touched him deeply and his emotions were kicking in for the first time in a long time. Every time he'd sung a song this afternoon, an image of her brushing at her eyes had stayed with him. Something had upset her.

He closed his eyes, touched the stone at the gate and let the rush take him home.

As he entered the back gate to his garden, the tantalising smell of Italian herbs wafted past. Before he could change his mind, he put his guitar on the bench on his back porch and walked around to the rear of Violet Cottage. Logic told him not to go, but he couldn't help himself.

Megan was sitting at the table on the patio surrounded by a pile of papers. David stood watching quietly as she bent her head and wrote in a notebook. Her hair was damp and ringlets were plastered to her forehead. Her shoulders were bare, her skin almost translucent in the soft light, and the same perfume she'd worn in his car today wafted across to him. It mingled with the perfume of the roses spilling over the fence between the cottages. As he stepped towards her, she frowned and pursed her lips, tapping the pen on the table. She lifted her head and looked at him without speaking as he stood by the table.

"I just came over to check on your water, but it looks like you've found a plumber?" He pointed to her damp hair.

She shook her head. "No, a guy called Ned dropped off a big container of water and lugged it into the bathroom for me. I managed to heat enough on the stove to have a much-needed bath."

"I'll have a look at the well for you now."

"The well?"

"Yes, the water to both houses comes from a well in the backyard of your cottage."

"So have you got water?" she asked.

"I do."

Megan laughed and her whole face came alive. He couldn't stop looking at her. Her eyes were suddenly

102

bright and for the first time he noticed the fleck of gold in her green irises. Unable to resist, he lifted both hands so that her face was framed in his fingers. She held his gaze and smiled.

"What? What's so funny?" he asked.

"I was starting to believe the stories of the woman in the village shop." She shook her head and he dropped his hands away. "She had me convinced it was something to do with the solstice."

"Nah, more to do with the cottage being empty and the pump seizing up. Jules is an old hippie. She's been here since the first Glastonbury festival." He turned his head away, realizing he'd given away too much with that simple observation. He had to learn to hold his tongue, as well as keep his hands off her. She hadn't moved when he'd held her face. Now, he sniffed appreciatively and glanced across at the stove. "I'll go down and check the pump for you if I can share your dinner. How's that for a deal?"

"Sounds fair to me."

"Pizza?"

"Sorry, just spaghetti sauce." Her face was guarded and his heart did a strange little jump as she dropped her gaze.

Whoa, what was that? I haven't felt a rush like that for a long while.

Pushing the feeling away, he flickered a glance across the papers on the table as he turned to head down towards the well. "Your research?"

"Not really, just a problem I have to sort out."

***

Megan had gathered the sheets of paper together when David arrived. It had been demoralising reading the e-mail from Tony about supposed dates that she had allegedly opened, read, and deleted the e-mails from the vice-chancellor containing the allegations. With it was an audit trail of marks changed in the grade centre under her log-in name. Statements from two students who were prepared to say she had accepted money from them for high marks. And it went on and on…

She shook her head as she followed David, touching her face where his fingers had held her so gently. Her skin was tingling and alive, and the warmth of his fingers on her skin still lingered. For some strange reason, his touch had been welcome and it had been hard not to turn into his hand and put her lips against his fingers.

The grass was soft and cool beneath her bare feet and the dusk light was fading. A small measure of calm stole over her as she padded along behind him. David wore his usual black T-shirt and she had to strain to see where he was heading.

"Oh, look!" She smiled when a white rabbit hopped across the grass in front of her and stopped to nibble at the long grass close to her bare feet.

David stopped in front of her and she cannoned straight into him. He grabbed her arms to stop her from falling. She'd been focused on the small white fluffy creature and hadn't been watching where she was going. His hard chest was warm against her cheek and for a moment, she rested her head there, listening to the steady thump of his heart. Megan closed her eyes and took a deep breath before she pulled away from him.

What the hell am I doing?

"Sorry, I was looking at the rabbit," she muttered, feeling a bit like Alice in Wonderland. "So, where's this well?"

David stood looking down at her and when he spoke his deep voice sent a ripple curling through her stomach. "Why are you so sad, Megan?"

"I'm not," she said tersely. "I'm just keen to get the water fixed so I can get settled and get on with my work." There was no way she was sharing her worries with a stranger. And he *was* a stranger, no matter how kind he was being now, and how much his touch stirred her. Since he'd lost the macho rock-star act and been civil to her, he'd been a different person. And his resemblance to the idol of her dreams still threw her every time he spoke to her. It would be very interesting to hear him perform and see if he sounded anything like his uncle.

She stepped away. "So where is it?"

Chapter Nine

Fixing the water had been a simple matter. No one had told Megan about the switch on the pump on the side of the well. In fact, she really knew nothing about the cottage apart from the fact that it belonged to Beth's family. Despite being old and using a well, it turned out there was a surprisingly modern electrical setup to send water through the yard to the house.

Letting the icy cold water run into the sink until the rust cleared, Megan turned to David but looked away immediately, not wanting to meet the piercing dark gaze that was fixed on her face. Her skin prickled and she ignored the rapid beat of her heart.

His resemblance to Davy Morgan unnerved her.

That was the explanation for the crazy feelings that surged through her every time she looked at him, or when he spoke, and when he'd touched her. The warmth and the tightness in her chest were the same as when she gave herself over to the flow of music. Nothing to do with the muscular chest outlined by the tight T-shirt or the fine dusting of hair on his forearms as she lowered her glance. It was bad enough that his speaking voice sent goosebumps skittering down her back. It was so deep and melodious, that he could just imagine what it sounded like when he sang.

"What sort of music does your band play?" Her voice croaked and she cleared her throat.

Focus. Change the subject. Anything to ignore his gaze.

"Ah…" He crossed his arms and turned away and relief coursed through Megan as he looked at the water gushing from the tap in the sink. As he spoke, she moved back to the sink to turn it off.

"We do covers of…er…Davy's work. He's still popular over here in the UK, you know." He seemed a bit defensive about playing the old songs and Megan rushed in to reassure him, although she was disappointed to hear he only played his uncle's covers and nothing original.

"Oh, he's still big in Australia too. Even though it's seventies music, you'll hear at least one of his songs played on the radio every day." She grasped the tap to turn it off, but nothing happened. Reaching over with her other hand, she grasped it firmly and twisted hard but the cold water continued to stream out. "In fact, I was watching a show on the trip over and there he was, Davy Morgan on the small screen in an aeroplane."

Megan froze as sudden warmth along her back alerted her to David's proximity, and his hand covered hers on the tap as he leaned close. She glanced up sideways from beneath her lashes, but his attention was fixed on the tap. The pressure of his fingers pinched her thumb against the old porcelain tap.

"Ouch."

He let go but didn't step back. "Here, I'll do it."

Megan raised her hands but couldn't move away as she was pinned between him and the sink. As he strained to shut off the tap, the tops of his arms pressed into her shoulders and she focused on looking through the window into the dark garden. The hard length of his body against her back and her legs, and the warmth it was generating against her bare shoulders, set her legs trembling.

The water shut off but he stayed where he was. His hand brushed softly against the side of her neck and she closed her eyes.

"You've got some rose petals caught in your hair." His voice was low and throaty and close to her ear and she reached up to rub her hand through her hair before turning to face him.

Still, he didn't move.

Megan swallowed and stared up into his deep blue eyes. Each of his dark eyelashes was clearly defined and he stared back at her steadily. Her heart slowed down and dropped to a steady beat and she waited for him to kiss her.

He leaned forward and his warm breath brushed her face like the touch of a butterfly wing. His hands gently held her shoulders and he lowered his head a touch closer.

"Are you going to feed me?"

Stepping back, she bit her lip as heat suffused her face. *How stupid am I? Why would he kiss someone like me?*

"Yes, of course." Reaching back, she grabbed her hair and twisted it into a knot to give herself something to do besides look at David. He moved across to the table and pulled a chair out and straddled it backward.

"Have you got any wine?"

Megan glanced across at the cupboard and laughed to break the tension. "No, I didn't carry any in my suitcase, and if you look in the cupboard, you'll find two apples and a bottle of water. The sauce bubbling in that saucepan is the sum total of my shopping this afternoon."

"Haven't you discovered the cellar?"

"Cellar?" Megan hadn't seen anything resembling a cellar. "What cellar?"

"The wine stash."

She laughed again. "No, but I haven't been here long enough to have a good look around. I was too busy trying to get the water going."

"You don't have to look far." David pushed himself up off the chair and held out his hand. Megan looked at it for a moment before slipping her hand into his, and he pulled her across to the corner of the kitchen beside the old Welsh dresser. "Before she died, I used to help Alice out with a few chores and she always gave me a bottle of wine." Megan tried to ignore the shocks running from her hand up her arm. Bloody star-struck, that's what she was.

"Ready?" He quirked an eyebrow and Megan tried not to stare. The resemblance to his uncle was really amazing. She wondered if his father had been Davy's twin. David tugged at her hand and she jumped.

"Daydreaming?"

"No." She shook her head slowly. "I just can't get over how much you look like *the* Davy Morgan."

He shrugged and gave her a tight smile. "Well, I'm *the* current David Morgan, anyway."

"Sorry, that probably came out rudely. I meant—" He waved her protest away before she could finish and pointed to the wall.

She hadn't noticed the low door set in the wall next to the dresser. It was painted the same bright yellow as the kitchen walls and was hidden in a dark

111

corner away from the window. A small circular handle, in the same yellow, was on the top of the door. David dropped her hand and pulled at it and the door came open with a creaking groan. As he bent down, Megan crouched next to him and peered in. A dark narrow space ran the length of the wall and it was just high enough to step in if you bent your head.

For her anyway; he was too tall and wide to fit in.

He stepped back and gestured to the cellar. "Do you want to choose a bottle of wine to go with that delectable-smelling sauce?"

"Is it okay to use one, do you think?" Megan stepped in and squealed as a cobweb drifted down onto her face. She brushed it away and peered around in the dim light. Dozens of bottles lined the walls, all covered in a fine layer of dust. She reached up for one and coughed as the dust flew up into the air.

"Seeing as Alice has gone, I am sure she won't mind." His deep voice followed her in. "And the family rarely stays here."

"Who looks after the cottage? Beth—my friend who offered me the cottage—didn't tell me much about it."

David reached over for the bottle Megan held in her hand and waited for her to step out of the small space.

While he closed the door, Megan went over to the stove and stirred the tomato sauce before filling another pot with water for the pasta. She turned the tap on carefully, relieved when the water shut off on the first go.

David wiped the wine bottle on his jeans before placing it on the table. "Alice was a bit of an eccentric. I met her…a few years back when I first bought the cottage and she liked to have company. I used to look after the garden for her when I was here, and I've just kept it up. The cottage is empty most of the time now."

"The woman in the shop told me she haunts the cottage."

David stared at her for a moment before his face creased into a huge grin. "Did she now? Don't worry about Jules. I think she smoked a bit too much of the happy weed in her time. She's a relic from the seventies. New age spiritual beliefs, and all that. You know, back in the seventies the villagers put up signs about hippies not being welcome in the shops and cafés in town." David laughed but he looked away and didn't meet her gaze. He picked up the wine bottle and looked at the label. "Alice was quite partial to a good drop."

Megan wandered over to the table and looked at the bottle he was holding up.

"Oh my God, we can't drink that. What a waste with a pack of bolognaise sauce." She did her best to read the label in her schoolgirl French accent. *"Château Fombrauge 1971 Grand Cru Classé de Saint Emilion."* She put her hands on her hips. "1971!"

"A good year." David smiled at her.

"It must be worth a fortune."

"If it bothers you so much, I'll replace it next time I go up to the city." Megan looked at him curiously. He mustn't be too much of a struggling artist if he could afford to replace a bottle of wine that old. She knew enough to know it must be worth a few hundred dollars—pounds—at least.

"Well, if you're sure the family wouldn't mind…and if you're going to replace it." Megan scrabbled in the drawer by the sink for a corkscrew and then watched as David pierced the cork with the metal prong. She kept her gaze on his fingers as he wound the corkscrew, slowly round and round. His hands were slender and she could see the rough callouses on the pads of his fingers from playing his guitar. Her breath caught as she imagined those rough fingers caressing her skin.

Turning away, she went across to the stove and busied herself tipping the pasta into the bubbling water, and she blamed the rising steam for the heat in her face.

God, what is wrong with me? If he sings I'll probably go into a quivering heap. She'd never been so physically affected by the mere presence of a man before.

By the time she'd served the meal, David had found some large crystal goblets and poured the cherry-red wine into them.

"To you, Megan." He raised his glass and waited for her to lift hers to clink on his. "May your holiday and your visit to the festival be everything you dreamed."

She lifted the glass to her lips and sipped, closing her eyes as the luscious fruity flavour fizzed on her tongue before sliding smoothly down her throat. Instant warmth hit her stomach and she opened her eyes to meet his gaze.

"Beautiful." His voice was soft and he held her eyes with his as he sipped from the crystal. Confusion filled her at his ambiguity and she decided to assume he was talking about the wine. Her guard went up and she put the goblet down on the table. Her feelings were erratic enough without enhancing them with wine.

"It is." Reaching for the steaming bowl in the centre of the table, she held it out to David and he served the pasta onto both of their plates.

"It's a fairly basic meal to eat with such a good wine." She grinned at him and returned the conversation to the mundane. "I am sure the French winemaker would be horrified to know it was accompanying a dried pasta sauce."

They ate silently for a few moments and Megan racked her brain to think of something, anything, to fill the awkward silence.

"Tell me about your music. You said you just do covers?" She cradled her face in one hand while she sipped at the wine. She'd just finish this glass. "Tell me how you came into music. Is it a hobby for you or a profession?"

She stared at him, waiting for his answer, blaming the breathless feeling in her chest on the potent wine.

"Music is my life," he said. "It is as necessary to me as the air I breathe and the food I eat. I couldn't survive without it." He held her gaze and his eyes darkened. "I have written many…many of my own songs too."

Megan sat up straight, her interest piqued. It seemed important to him that she knew he played more than covers of Davy Morgan's songs. Her fingers itched to write down the words he'd said about

116

music being his life. It would make a great quote in her work. "So, you've been to a few Glastonbury festivals?"

"Yes, a few," he said.

"Have you noticed a change in the crowds there through the years?" Putting her wine down on the table, she leaned forward. "What I am looking at in my doctorate is the sociological impact of rock festivals on society. I believe the type of people who attend seems to have changed as the festivals have become more organised. I suppose, what I mean is, the festivals have turned into more of a moneymaking concern over the years."

David's mouth tightened and he stared past her. "Being a musician, I'm focused on the music, and I really don't know the demographic the festival attracts. But I do believe there always has been...shall we say... a tendency to 'glorify' the musicians to sell more records." He lifted his glass to the light and swirled the wine around. "For me, it's like this wine. We enjoy drinking good wine...the taste, the physical effect it has on us. That's how I see my music."

"'Records'? That's an old-fashioned term to use." Megan tipped her head to the side. "Do you agree that the people who attended the early festivals were more true lovers of music than those who go now? My research seems to indicate that it has become trendy to attend festivals now, and there seems to be a huge commercial push behind it. Geared to selling 'records' as you say, rather than just making music like the old days? Musicians seem to be more of a commodity these days—from as far back as the seventies."

"I'm just a simple musician, sweetheart." David shook his head. "I play music. I do it for me. The rush I get when the synergy comes together is as good as the best sex I've ever had."

He leaned back in his chair and pinned her with his gaze.

"Speaking of which…"

Chapter Ten

Megan's questions were straying into territory David didn't want to enter. He could kick himself for the slip- ups he'd made. "Records" and telling her he wrote his own music. Bloody trying to impress her. Jesus, she was damned beautiful and unaware of it. She was sucking him in without even trying. Getting close to her, or any other woman, was the last thing he intended to do.

So, he pulled out the macho rock-star act again. It had the immediate effect he expected from her. She sat up straight in her chair and her face closed.

"I think the deal was—you fix the pump and I give you dinner?" Her voice was like ice.

"Can't blame a guy for trying." He stood and carried his plate across to the sink. "It was very pleasant chatting with you, but I've got some work to do, if I can't interest you in a bit of fun?"

"Thanks for fixing the pump for me." Megan walked to the door and opened it. "And for showing me the cellar."

His words had had the desired effect. Her face was closed and she folded her arms across her chest. David tucked his thumbs into his jeans pockets as a craving to pull her close overtook him. She looked up at him silently, wide-eyed, and if he knew women, the look on her face was hunger.

And not for food.

But she surprised him with her next words. "If you think your resemblance to your uncle is going to have me jumping joyfully into your bed, it will take a lot more than that."

"What will it take?" he asked softly.

He wasn't certain who moved first but her lips brushed lightly against his. David groaned, took his hands from his pockets and pulled her hard against him. Soft skin, hot mouth, and the subtle scent he was beginning to associate with her flooded him with wanting. Sounds of pleasure vibrated against his mouth and his body quivered as he felt her heart racing against his. He moved his mouth lower and kissed the spot that was pulsing frantically. Her skin was warm and she relaxed against him, and he closed his eyes, taking pleasure in her soft skin as he slid his lips up the long line of her throat until he pressed his mouth against hers.

Megan drew back from him but still stood within his arms. Her cheeks were flushed. She trailed her fingers across her lips and the blood surged to his groin. The taste of her mouth stayed on his lips.

"You'd better go and do that work you said you had to do." She stepped back and smiled at him. "I might see you tomorrow. I'm going to wander over and check out the festival."

***

Megan walked upstairs and crossed to the window overlooking David's cottage. She watched as his lights came on and she leaned her head against the window. She looked out into the soft moonlight as his music filtered up to her. He was playing his uncle's songs again. Warmth settled low in her belly and she touched her lips as the music swelled and surrounded her. Closing her eyes, she took a deep breath as the fragrance of the garden drifted in through the window. Her body hummed with the music and the sweet smells, and she smiled as contentment filled her.

No man had ever had this effect on her before. It had to be the music. She crossed to the small bathroom adjacent to the bedroom and turned the taps on to fill the bath. She quickly went back down to the kitchen and cleared the table. Picking up the glass David had drunk from, she put it against her lips, almost regretting she had sent him home.

But it was too soon. She barely knew him.

##

Megan slept deeply but her dreams were filled with music again, and she woke late the next morning. Determined to go to the festival today, she dressed quickly and hurried down to the kitchen. Making herself a cup of tea, she wandered out through the utility room to the garden, picking up an old-fashioned crocheted hat from the hook beside the door and tucking her hair up beneath it. Her phone had charged overnight, and Megan glanced at the time on the screen before she slipped it into her pocket. It would be late evening at home in Australia. A chat with her sister would settle her. Perhaps it would get rid of these dreamy feelings that she couldn't seem to shake. And then she'd be in the right frame of mind to talk to Tony and discuss his e-mail.

She walked slowly through the flowers and sipped her tea, allowing her worries at home to take up only a tiny corner of her mind. The bees settled in the centre of the fat yellow roses, and the hollyhocks nodded as the butterflies flitted past. She touched the different flowers lightly as she walked past. She knew the names of them because her maternal grandmother had instilled a love of gardening in her, but it was difficult to indulge that love in an apartment in the city. Lavender, magnolias, delphiniums, and marigolds— the garden was a riot of colour and sweet fragrance.

She'd love to be able to afford to live somewhere like this for a while.

As she reached the back corner of the garden, the sound of the creaking gate from the cottage next door caught her attention. Her heart rate kicked up a beat as she watched David stride through the field towards the tents she could see in the far distance. Dressed in tight black jeans and a black T-shirt with his dark curls tumbling over his shoulders, he wore the same signature outfit his uncle used to wear. His guitar was slung over one shoulder and a small kit bag over the other. He looked like he had stepped straight from one of the old posters that had hung on the wall of her bedroom years ago. She kept her gaze fixed on him to see which way he went. If she took that route through the fields, it would be miles shorter than going around the road to Pilton.

As she watched, David stopped by a large stone post that stood in the centre of the field. He reached out to it and it looked as though he was trying to get his balance. He leaned over and his guitar swung around from his right shoulder as he pitched forward and disappeared.

Megan gasped and dropped her teacup to the grass. She ran across to the back gate of Violet Cottage, keeping her gaze fixed on the place where David had collapsed.

She pulled out her phone from her jeans pocket, trying to remember whether you dialled 911 or triple zero for medical assistance in England. Briefly dropping her gaze to the phone, she swore. It didn't matter anyway; she had no service.

Megan ran across the soft grass towards the spot where he'd fallen. A couple of cows mooed from the field on the other side of the fence and she glanced across, hoping they couldn't get into this field.

The stone post was only a hundred yards ahead now and she put her hand up to shade her eyes to see if David was sitting up. But she couldn't see him. He must have fallen on the other side. Her chest was hurting as she caught her breath, but she kept running.

What the hell should I do? Her first aid knowledge was minimal and there was no one for miles to call for help. What if he'd had a heart attack or something? She didn't know the first thing about CPR.

A small brook ran through the middle of the field and she reached down and removed her sandals, gasping as the icy water covered her feet. The grass was muddy on the other side and she dropped her shoes, intending to collect them on the way back.

The huge stone loomed in front of her. It was much higher than it appeared from the cottage. Dark-grained and made of a blue stone, the height and shape reminded her of the totem poles she had seen when she'd visited the States a couple of years back. She touched it as she peered around it, looking for David, but she pulled her hand back quickly. It was warm from the sun and almost vibrated beneath her hand.

Megan stopped and looked around. There was no sign of him. He must have fallen farther away but from her perspective, it had seemed as though it was here, at this post.

She shook her head as she remembered how he had been touching the stone when she had seen him fall. He had to be lying on the ground around here somewhere.

"David?" She put her hands up to her mouth and called but was met by silence. "Can you hear me?"

Nothing. The air was still and even the cows had quieted.

Circling the stone without touching it, she kept her eyes fixed on the ground. Stepping away, she scanned the field around her. There was no sign of him on the ground, nor was he walking between her and the tents that were only a couple of fields away.

The air rippled as she stepped back towards the stone.

Where the hell was he? Was he all right?

Megan glanced across the field and took a deep breath. There was another smaller stone farther to the

125

west. She must have come across to the wrong one. A soft humming filled her ears as she strode towards the second stone and suddenly, another smaller stone appeared out of nowhere and loomed in front of her. The grass was cold beneath her bare feet and goose bumps prickled her thighs.

"David, where are you?" Her words came out in a thin scream and she wiped her trembling hands down the front of her jeans as she walked in a straight line between the markers. She reached the final stone and peered around it.

There was no sign of him. Reaching out, she placed her palm flat against the huge rock and pulled back sharply as the cold bit into her skin. Panic swirled inside her as her vision faded and the humming she had heard at the other stone filled her ears.

I'm going to faint.

She dropped to her knees and lowered her head so the blood rushed downward but it made no difference. Cold shudders racked through her and sapped her strength and she held her hand out in front of her face. She was fading and she could see through the skin. Her hand was almost translucent, waving and shimmering as though it was beneath the water.

What's happening to me?

A strange feeling filled her, as though her bones and sinews loosened. She gripped the hat on her head, touching and squeezing the stiff cotton to ground herself.

I'm all right. I'm not going to pass out. Breathe.

Slippery connections held her together, loose and fragile. It was as though her body was stretching, shrinking, and disintegrating. She fought the cold feeling that was overtaking her limbs and tried to look around. Suddenly her airways relaxed, and as her lungs flooded with cool air, she pitched forward into the soft, damp grass.

Chapter Eleven

"Come on, Davy boy. Snap out of it." Bear was sitting at the drums with his beefy arms poised, waiting for him to launch into the riff of their opening song. He'd missed the cue to start. For the third time in the last half hour.

David couldn't understand the unease that was prickling at his neck. Sure, he'd gone to bed frustrated last night and couldn't get Megan out of his head, but that didn't explain the feeling that something was wrong. It had nagged at him ever since he'd arrived at the stage an hour ago. Holly had been talking to Bear when David had arrived but she'd taken off as soon as she'd seen him. She'd been avoiding him and his suspicions kicked in. He was getting used to the way she operated and he knew she was up to something.

But if she stayed away from him, he wouldn't have to watch his temper. He was quite happy to build their reputation by playing as much as they could and didn't need the sensational media coverage she insisted on. He'd talk to the guys about replacing her.

"You don't want to miss the cue tonight or we'll get booed off the stage. What the fuck's wrong with you, man?" The usually placid drummer glared at David and Slim nodded at him from the other side of the stage as he fiddled with the volume control on his bass guitar.

"Sorry. I'm not focused." David glanced across at Bear and lifted his guitar. "Take it from the top again."

He let the music wash over him as he tried to block the unease filling his mind. Technically he knew his playing was perfect, but the synergy just wasn't here today. He swallowed and closed his eyes, trying to get into the music, but his muse had disappeared.

He loved it when the music dripped from his fingers like honey, and he could lose himself in the rise and swell of the notes. But today he was just playing. Mechanical. Note followed note. It would sound the same to most people listening, but the magic had gone for him. He knew his heart wasn't there. Hopefully, it would be back for their first set when the festival kicked off at sunset. He wondered whether Megan had gotten over to her festival and whether she'd gone looking for him. He'd have to come up with some excuse about why the band wasn't there.

Bear looked across at him and David launched into their second song, letting the words fill his head.

Forget about her.

He noticed Slim and Bear exchanging a glance and he pulled himself together, making a last-ditch effort for the band. He closed his eyes and finally, the words vibrated in his chest, true and clear, and he was back into it. The small disquiet still niggled at him but he pushed it away.

Chapter Twelve

A hot breath stirred against her cheek and Megan turned her head into David's face, parting her lips softly to take his kiss. Her eyes opened slowly and confusion filled her as she looked into a white-tented wall.

Not David?

In her dream, he had been lying next to her on the soft grass and his hands had been touching her face with feather-light strokes.

"Are you with us now, darlin'?"

A pair of concerned brown eyes came into her view as she slowly lifted her head.

"What did you take?"

"What did I take?"

"Yeah, we think you must have had a bad trip. A couple of guys found you out in the field. You weren't eating those mushrooms, were you?"

"What mushrooms? I only had a cup of tea." Slowly Megan became aware of two men in some sort of medical uniforms hovering over her. She was in a tent and loud music slammed in through the opening.

She sat up and put her hands over her ears. They were buzzing.

The two men exchanged a glance and the younger one passed her a glass of cold water. She took it and drank deeply, grateful for the cool liquid sliding down her parched throat.

"Where am I?"

"At the Glastonbury festival. This is the St. John's first aid tent. You've been out of it for a few hours. The doctor checked you out earlier but he didn't want to send you to the hospital because they're out of room over there. He said to keep an eye on you and let you sleep it off."

"We've got some questions for you before we can let you go."

Megan nodded.

"First off, sweetheart, what's your name?"

"Megan Miller."

"Do you know the date?"

She squeezed her eyes closed. "It's the first day of the festival so I guess it's the 26th June."

"Good girl, Last question. What's your address?"

"In England or in Australia?"

"Here." Her thoughts were getting back into some sort of order and the dull headache had eased.

"The McLaren place. Violet Cottage, just across the field."

"Done good, love. Up you hop."

A loud crash of drums and guitars came in through the open flap and the older man frowned. "Davy Morgan's band is about to play. I swear they're the loudest here. Hate that modern music."

The young guy laughed. "But the young girls love him, Reg. We'll have the next wave of them swooning and passing out within the hour. You mark my words."

Megan followed the exchange with confusion as the events of the morning flooded her mind. "David Morgan's here? And his band is playing?" She swung her legs off the side of the bed. "He's all right, then?"

"Aye, he's all right," the man called Reg said. "He's been caterwauling that newfangled music out there all afternoon. You're lucky you slept through it, love."

Megan stood carefully as the young man held on to her arm. He passed her the hat she'd grabbed from the hook this morning. "You had no shoes on when you came in, but you should be able to get a pair of those rope sandals at one of them hippie stalls."

"You watch what you're doing out there, young lady." Reg towered over her with his hands on his hips and a stern look on his face. "We don't want to see you in here again. You feeling okay now?"

133

"Yes, thank you. I'm fine." Megan looked down at her bare feet. Her jeans were muddy around the bottom, but her clothes were dry. "I'm just going to go home. Honestly, I didn't take anything. I must have fainted."

Maybe it was delayed jet lag? Or it could have been that vintage wine we drank last night?

Maybe it was all a dream? But when she turned, Megan knew she was awake and this was real. She stepped towards the opening in the tent and turned back to the two men before leaving. "Thank you for taking care of me."

Their attention was already on another woman lying on a stretcher on the other side of the room and the young man lifted one hand in a brief wave. Megan lifted the tent flap and stepped outside. It was almost dusk and the rays of the setting sun lit up Glastonbury Tor in the distance.

The quirky voice of one of her favourite artists from the seventies, Melanie Safka, drifted across to her in the still evening air. The words of the song "Brand New Key" sounded out in a melancholy wave. Either they were piping in recorded music or whoever was singing was a brilliant cover artist. Megan looked around curiously. The festival was nowhere near as crowded as she'd expected, apart from a large group of people gathered around a pyramid of scaffolding on the other side of the field. As the song faded away, a bright orange flash lit the night sky and strident guitar chords blared out. Clouds of smoke billowed above the stage as the sun slipped below the horizon in a brilliant shaft of gold.

The ground was muddy outside the tent and she looked around, trying to figure out the way back to Violet Cottage. She was still confused and unsure of what had happened. Her feet were bare, she had no money on her or her festival ticket, and she'd left the house unlocked. As soon as she could figure out which direction to go, she'd head home. Turning around, she looked across the dark field but couldn't see any lights in the distance. A group of people came up the path behind her, and she was jostled across the grass towards the pyramid stage.

"Oh, man, how cool is that." The man beside her grabbed her arm and pointed, as another huge orange flare lit up the sky. "Look, working with the universe, man."

Megan shook his hand from her arm and hung back as they walked past her. The men all had shoulder-length hair and two of the women were wearing nothing from the waist up.

It was nothing like any of the rock festivals she'd been to in Australia. She wished she had her bag and camera with her to take notes and photos. Then she remembered her Smartphone in her pocket. Pulling it out, she tried to turn it on but the battery must have gone dead again because the screen stayed dark and blank when she pushed the buttons.

This festival was casual, nothing like the slick barricaded events she'd attended at home. She hoped they wouldn't ask to see her ticket on the way out as she had nothing with her apart from the cotton hat now scrunched up in her hand.

That's if I can find the way out. More people were coming up the path and she was jostled closer to the stage as they pushed past her. The smell of dope was overpowering and there was not a security person in sight.

"Peace, man."

"Love, man."

The words echoed around her as the throngs of festival-goers headed towards the stage. The voice of her favourite singer sounded loud and pure through the huge speakers suspended from the top of the pyramid.

Megan pushed her way through to the front of the crowd. Her attention was totally focused on the familiar voice in front of her, and she elbowed and jostled until she could see the band. The music was deafening and the beat reverberated in her chest.

Bright lights glared down from the stage, and she put her hand to her eyes as the lights blinded her for a moment. The noise was incredible. She dropped her hand to her side and looked up at the stage.

David stood with his eyes closed and his lips caressing the microphone as the words and voice of his uncle, Davy Morgan, came from his mouth. Megan closed her eyes and swayed with the music. His voice was identical and the song was one she knew by heart.

It could have been Davy Morgan himself.

***

David got to the end of the first line of the song and looked down at the crowd in front of the stage. A mass of waving, swaying bodies, bright eyes, and bare chests filled his vision under the bright spotlight at the side. Most of the women had skimpy tops on...if they had a top on at all. There was more than one flash of bare boobs and he grinned across at Slim.

Slim was in his element. The bass guitarist was a breast man through and through.

As David belted out the words at the end of the second verse, his gaze settled on a face he recognised. His eyes widened in disbelief as the shock hit him like a truck

Oh, fuck, fuck, fuck.

He recovered and kept singing but his chest closed as tension gripped his muscles.

Please God, let me be wrong.

Moving forward to the centre of the stage, he looked down at the woman who'd caught his attention.

Hell and damnation. It *was* Megan. Gazing up at him, her mouth was open, her face pale...but her expression was full of awe and adoration. Her head turned as though she sensed him looking at her, and as her gaze locked with his, a sweet smile brought her face alive.

David couldn't take his eyes from her face as the blood pushed through his veins in a slow thumping surge. The pace of the music picked up and he kept singing even though time had come to a grinding halt.

Don't leave me, stay with me,

I will love you forever

Through time itself.

He sang the words without thinking about them until he reached the end of the chorus.

How fucking appropriate. Except for the bit about love.

How the hell had the woman from the twenty-first century turned up here in front of him at the fucking 1971 Glastonbury Festival? She had bewitched him and now he had a major problem on his hands. She must have known about the stones all along. He spun around at the end of the song, caught Bear's eyes, and nodded towards Megan.

Bear's eyes widened and he mouthed back at David. "How the fuck did she get here?"

David shrugged, and Bear launched into the drum roll that began the final song of their set.

David closed his eyes. Sweat soaked his shirt and the usual gimmick at the end of the last song was to pull his shirt off and throw it to the crowd.

This is going to be the performance of my life.

He took a deep breath, cleared his mind of everything but the song, and let the words fill his soul. The music dropped off and a hush fell over the crowd. They knew what was coming. Slim hit the guitar pedal and a series of long mournful notes hovered in the air. David stepped to the front of the stage and let the microphone stand go as he slowly peeled his shirt off and threw it into the crowd. A roar from below filled his ears as the drums kicked in. He picked up his guitar and looped the strap around his neck as Slim hit the deep notes on his bass guitar. The music reverberated through the night air and surged through his blood. Heat filled him from within and he had never felt more alive than he did at that moment. The night, the people, and the pulsating music joined in one wave and he was at one with the universe. The muse was back and the synergy among the band, the music, the words, and the crowd was complete.

Pure, clean energy filled him. The connection had been made.

He reached the end of the chorus and a euphoric haze filled him. David stopped singing and let his gaze drop to Megan. The noise from the crowd surged as they sang the words.

Her eyes were fixed on him and her cheeks were flushed. Joy filled her expression and he realised that she felt it, too. Picking up the microphone, he sang the next verse. A shaft of pure sexual desire ran through him and his feelings poured out through the words of the song and the crowd roared in appreciation as he gyrated on the stage.

One final spin and the words died away with the music. David reached out and brushed his fingers across the dozens of hands stretching across the front of the stage as he ran from left to right. He paused when he came to where Megan stood.

He knelt down on one knee and held his hand out to her, calling loudly over the noise of the crowd.

"Don't move. Stay right here." She looked up at him and he squeezed her fingers between his.

"I'll be down in less than five minutes," he said.

She nodded, her dark eyes glittering with emotion.

David waved to the crowd as Bear gave one final drum roll and the next band moved on to the stage. The lead singer from Fairport Convention grabbed the microphone and yelled to the crowd. "Hey, guys and gals, do Davy Morgan and his band rock or what?"

A huge cheer went up as the crowd chanted for more and David took the microphone back for a moment. "More later. We're back on in the morning," he promised with a wave. "Don't go away."

He looked across at Bear and passed him his guitar as he ran off the stage and headed for the steps.

God, Megan, don't move. How the bloody hell did you get here?

For the life of him, he had no idea how she had found the gate. But she obviously had. Had the McLarens told her? Alice must have told her family about it, although she had sworn no one else knew. And now he had to get her back to the cottage before dawn and find his way back to the festival because it was bloody hard to find the correct lines and markers at the wrong time of day—as he'd discovered a few nights ago when he had come home to find Megan on his porch. Dawn, dusk, and midday were the easiest, if not the only, times to cross through the time gate.

"There's no way she can stay. If she gets lost, I'll never find her and she'll never find her way back by herself." Panicked, he tore down the steps.

"David, wait."

He stopped dead as Holly appeared and grabbed his arm. "Not now. I have to go."

"I have to talk to you." Holly's eyes were unfocused as she stared at him and her words were slightly slurred. "It's real important."

He looked down at her and she raised her hands to grab each side of his face. "David, you were beautiful. You did yourselves…the best…the best…"

David lifted her hands away. "Later, Holly."

Before he could move away, she pushed into him and her hands were on the front of his pants. "You have gotten me so hot, David." She'd never spoken to him like that before. Despite his disapproval of her publicity ideas, they'd always maintained a professional relationship.

"What the fuck are you on, Holly?" He narrowed his eyes as he looked down at her. Her pupils were dilated and she stared past him.

"Have you being smoking dope?" He grasped her arms, and led her to the stairs he'd just come down. Seconds later, Bear appeared at the top.

"Mate, look after her, will you? I've got to go and find Megan before she disappears."

Holly was with it enough to glare at him. "Who's Megan?"

David didn't answer as he handed her over to Bear and he took off as the electric folksy music of Fairport Convention began to play. He ducked and weaved through the roaring crowd as hands reached out to him, but most of their attention was on the new band on the stage. His arms and chest were slick with the sweat running down his neck and face, and he reached up and pushed his hair back as it stuck to his brow and dropped across his eyes.

He stood at the side of the stage and anxiously scanned the crowds.

Thank the gods.

Her reddish hair stood out like a beacon against the bright light and he pushed his way through the crowd.

"Watch it, man." One of the concertgoers shoved him with his elbow as he tried to reach Megan but apologised as soon as he looked over at David.

"Oh, sorry. Hey, look girls, it's Davy Morgan."

David shook his head and grabbed Megan's arm. She turned to him, her face rapt. Twin spots of colour stained her cheeks and she reached up and wiped her tears away with a shaking hand. He took her hand firmly in his and cleared a path through the crowd. Silently he led her away from the solid mass of noise, behind the pyramid and towards the riverbank. Along the way they passed three couples on the ground, totally oblivious to the world, immersed in their own private activity.

Megan's soft gasp reached him in the darkness as she moved to the side before she stepped on a naked couple entwined on the grass in the middle of the path.

Finally, they were away from the noise and the crowd. The air was soft and still as they came to a stop beside the riverbank.

Megan looked up at him wordlessly and he held his arms out to her.

***

She leaned into David's bare chest. It was hot and slick with sweat. Closing her eyes, she felt safe for the first time since she'd fainted in the field this afternoon. It was like coming home. His strong arms held her close and the smell of sweat and stage makeup filled her senses. Finally, he spoke and his voice seemed guarded.

"How did you get here, Megan? Do you know about the stones?"

"Yes, I know the Stones are due here. What's that got to do with anything?" She stepped back from him and crossed her arms. A shiver went through her. Now that she was away from the excitement of the performance and out in the open air, the night was cool. She rubbed her hands up and down her arms as she looked up at David.

His face was closed, so different from the energy and life it had been filled with on the stage.

"He called you Davy Morgan." Confusion filled her. "Why did he call you Davy?"

David dropped his forehead against hers as he reached for her elbows and his warm breath fluttered her hair.

"Because that's who I am," he said simply.

"You do his songs so well. It is almost as though you *are* him."

Ice skittered through Megan's limbs as David lifted his head and looked out over the fields into the dark night.

"I have to get you home, Megan." His voice was quiet and distant. "Quickly."

Something was wrong and she didn't understand what was happening.

"Why?"

"Because you shouldn't be here."

"I know. I haven't even got my ticket or my stuff. I really didn't intend to come here. I followed you when you fell. I thought you'd taken ill. I was worried when I couldn't find you. And then I must have fainted because I woke up in the first aid tent." She reached her hand up to his face but he stepped back

145

and dropped his hands from her arms before her fingers reached his cheek. "But now that I'm here and I've heard the music, I want to stay. I can't miss a minute of this. It makes me feel so alive."

David turned away from her and the strong moonlight highlighted the proud line of his back as he stood bare-chested beside her. A surge of hot desire spiralled through her and settled low in her belly. It was like nothing she'd ever experienced before. Her heart beat in her throat, slow and steady as she searched for words, but they didn't come so she reached out and let her hands speak for her. She trailed her fingers from his shoulders slowly down his hot, damp skin until her fingers paused at the top of his tight black jeans. Ever since she had kissed him last night, she'd known this moment was inevitable.

His skin twitched beneath her fingers but still he didn't turn to her. She breathed in deeply and walked around to face him. Trailing her finger slowly down his bare chest from the base of his neck to the top of his jeans, her fingers lingered on the metal button at the top of the zipper and he dropped his head into her neck. She sighed as his hot lips moved down to her shoulder and he nipped at her skin with his teeth.

Pulling back, he muttered with a low groan. "I have to get you home, Megan."

"Soon." She would die if he didn't touch her. "After."

Now.

He pulled her deeper into the shadows next to the softly babbling water. They were alone and the noise of the concert was faint in the distance.

"I want you." His words were simple and she held his dark eyes with hers. The heat from his skin warmed Megan and pushed her further over the edge. There was no going back.

She sat on the soft grass and lifted her hands in invitation. David dropped beside her and gently cupped her face in his hands, as he had the other night. But this time, his gaze was searching hers and there was intent in his eyes. His strong face was outlined in the moonlight and the wild black curls formed a halo around his head as the moonlight shone from behind him. Megan turned her head to kiss his palm and murmured against his warm skin.

"What if someone comes along? We could find ourselves up on YouTube before the night is over."

David lifted his hand to cover hers and even her fingers tingled from his touch. "We're far enough away to be private, but don't worry. The solstice has played havoc with everyone's phone." He stared at her and his gaze was unwavering. "Trust me, no one will be taking photos with their phones here tonight."

His deep voice surrounded her and need rushed through her blood. She arched her head back and gripped his shoulders as the wonder of the night filled her. The sky was brilliant with stars, and the soft halo of light from the full moon spilled down onto David's loose curls. It was the most beautiful sight she'd ever seen.

Dropping her hands, she reached down to the hem of her T-shirt, pulled it up over her head, and dropped it on the ground before slowly getting to her feet. She stepped out of her jeans and stood before him, the moonlight bathing her skin with translucent light.

David knelt in front of her and lowered his head. His long curls gently brushed the tips of her nipples and she sensed he was holding back as his mouth pressed against her stomach. Megan held his head against her bare skin for a moment before she lowered herself to the grass. When he took her mouth with his with a gentle kiss, she opened to him and let her tongue slide against his as he deepened the pressure of his lips. For a full minute, she savoured the taste of him in her mouth, the warmth of his tongue, pushing and retreating. She drew a breath as his mouth moved along her cheek and caressed her ear before his lips blazed a hot trail down her neck.

"I want you, Megan. I shouldn't. But you are in my blood." His voice had roughened and held an edge of despair.

Megan's whole body throbbed and her inhibitions fled as raw power consumed her. Her desire matched his. She didn't care where she was, or if anyone could see her. Megan held David's gaze as she slipped off the brief wisp of lace that was all that remained between her and sheer, naked freedom. She lay back in the soft grass and watched as he shed his jeans. A shaft of pure heat pulsed through her as he stood in front of her. The moonlight caught his body, but his face was shadowed. He was ready for her. He lay next to her but she craved his hard weight on her, in her, and filling her...but he paused and wooed her with gentle fingers. Thoughts flitted through her mind, sensations touched her skin, and the ache deep within her grew as his gaze locked with hers. He moved his head closer to hers and the close resemblance he bore to the rock star she'd idolised growing up actually stole her breath away for a moment. The face, the eyes, the voice, the emotions she'd carried within every time she'd heard his songs. And now this man, David, was taking the place of those memories, and the feelings consuming her were like nothing she'd ever experienced.

Who was he and where were these feelings coming from?

"Touch me," she whispered and it came out with a sigh as she drew in a ragged breath.

Lightly circling around her nipples, his fingers teased her and she bit her lip. Her body ached, wanting him. Lighter circles around her stomach gradually trailed down to the fine hair between her thighs. She clenched her thighs, fighting the sweet sensations building and pulsing. In the distance, the music gentled and a soft, dreamy song drifted across to them.

"I need you." Her voice was full of the need pulsing through her. "Now."

He rolled on top of her with a groan and braced himself with his hands before plunging into her in one swift movement. An unfamiliar guttural sound came from her throat as she clenched around him. She rocked with him, lifting her hips in time with his thrusts, almost making their own music as the heat between them built to a crescendo. It rolled to one long glorious swell that gushed heat and music through her body and soul.

When their eyes met, she smiled and succumbed to him, giving in to the exquisite waves overtaking her as David groaned and buried his warm mouth in her neck.

Megan smiled and let his music take her under.

##

"Megan?" His voice was soft against her ear and she smiled.

"Mm?"

She savoured the slickness of David's hot and slippery skin on hers. A deep contentment filled her and she kept her eyes closed, not wanting to think about what had happened, but just to live in the moment and enjoy it.

But it had to end.

A cool breeze raised goose bumps on her skin as David pulled away and knelt beside her. His face was in the shadows and she couldn't see his expression.

But when he spoke his words were soft and calm. "I should apologise but I'm not going to. That was an amazing thing that just happened between us." He touched her shoulder and then gently ran his hand through her hair. "I want you to know, no matter what garbage I said at the cottage the other night, I don't do this."

"It was the most beautiful moment of my life. Did you feel the music?" Megan rolled to her side, untroubled by her nakedness. From the soft sounds drifting across to them, they were not alone in their pursuits of the night.

David looked around and picked up her shirt and passed it to her. "Yes, I did."

"It was a perfect setting. Tell me. Am I dreaming?" Her voice sounded dreamy to her and she rolled her T-shirt up and put it under her head. It was unlike her not to be self-conscious and she stretched, savouring the soreness of her muscles.

But as she stretched the physical tug of sensation broke into her dreamy state, and doubt seeped in.

Megan bit her lip. Had it all been a dream? Had she really experienced that sublime moment?

Has the whole day been one glorious dream?

"Did I just make the most beautiful love with David Morgan or am I dreaming of Davy Morgan?" Her voice was still dreamy and her eyelids were heavy. She couldn't keep them open much longer.

"No." David's voice broke into her sleepiness and reassured her. "That was for real. Are you okay?"

She opened her eyes and smiled up at him. "I just need a little nap."

He laid her jeans beside her. "I'll just go tell the guys I'm taking you…home…and then I'll be right back. Don't move. Okay?"

"Okay," she murmured sleepily and closed her eyes.

##

A blackbird trilled at the promise of dawn and Megan woke. Despite the cold, a pleasant languor filled her body but she looked down in confusion, covering herself with both hands.

Oh my God, I'm lying stark naked on the grass next to a stream. She sat up and looked around but there was no one in sight. She put on her shirt and knelt by the brook. After a quick wash with the cold water, she pulled her jeans back on. Her shoes were still back in the field by that huge rock and the pink hat was long gone. Bemused, she sat beside the babbling brook and waited for David. The sun climbed higher and touched the fields with the rosy glow of dawn, but he didn't come back.

Where was he? He'd told her to wait here, but she had no idea how long she'd slept or how long he'd been gone. She waited another few minutes before pushing herself to her feet. Following the brook, she wandered over a small hill. Music was still blaring from the stage, but a different band was playing. As she watched, she remembered being with David for most of the night, though time had lost all meaning for her.

But had they really been together or had she just dreamed about David?

Or Davy?

As she looked across the fields, her vision swam for a second, and the ground tipped beneath her feet. Had they given her some drug when she'd been in that tent earlier? Had she hallucinated? Megan shook her head in confusion, not knowing what was real or what was a dream.

She looked around through the crowds at the front of the stage, but there was no sign of David or his band. She'd recognised his drummer and the guitarist as the two men from the pub the other day.

As a shaft of golden light lit the stage in front of her, the music stopped and the voice of the announcer came scratchily through the loudspeaker.

"Ladies and gentlemen, I present to you David Bowie, who will herald in the dawn of the summer solstice."

Bloody hell. Megan turned around swiftly and the simple piano chords of an early David Bowie song drifted across to her as he encouraged all the sleepyheads to wake up.

She listened and shook her head in bemusement.

What a strange choice of a song for Bowie to play at Glastonbury 2011.

"Oh! You Pretty Things" was one of his songs from the early seventies and had never been that popular. In fact, it had been from before he'd hit the big time. And it must have been a last-minute decision to have him appear. He hadn't been on her ticket or in any of the promos she'd read about the festival.

What an amazing bonus.

She squinted.

It must be some sort of act or cover show? It couldn't be Bowie. The singer seated at the piano was dressed in seventies clothes and had a seventies wig on to emulate Bowie's early glamour look. She knew he'd played at one of the earliest Glastonbury concerts in the seventies—she'd come across that in her research. Maybe it was a re-creation for this festival?

But still, she listened and closed her eyes. The singer copied the song brilliantly. His rendition was perfect.

When the song ended, Megan stepped to the side and looked around for David. She had no idea where he had disappeared to but she was determined to settle in and enjoy the music. She was at Glastonbury and she wanted to enjoy every second, no matter what strange things had happened to her.

She'd heard terrific music, had vivid, crazy dreams, and had great sex...and she was not going back to the cottage until the music stopped...despite having bare feet and no money. Looking around, she grinned...she fit right in with the hippie crowd.

Chapter Thirteen

David cursed as he shoved through the group of people blocking the entrance to the large tent Holly had hired for them behind the stage. Finally, with much elbowing and muttering, he got past the crowd and entered the dim space. The sweet smell of dope met him and he frowned. Bear was sitting on a camp chair and Slim was asleep on the ground behind him.

"Did you bring my guitar down off stage?"

Bear inclined his head to the back of the tent. David walked over and reached for his guitar, which was resting on his kit bag.

"Thanks. Where's Holly?" He frowned at Bear and gestured to the joint between the drummer's fingers. "You know how I feel about that when we're performing."

Bear pointed to the corner of the tent. Holly was curled up on a blanket with her eyes closed. "Don't worry. Chill out, she's fine."

David put his guitar to one side and dug in his bag for a clean black T-shirt. "I'm taking Megan home."

"I thought you already had. Couldn't you find her? You've been gone for hours."

David pulled the shirt over his head. He was already regretting what had happened now that he was away from her. He turned away and spoke gruffly. "Yeah, took a while to find her."

Bear put the joint up to his mouth and inhaled deeply.

"Get rid of that. We're back on stage in a couple of hours." David lifted up the flap of the tent. "And look after Holly."

"Who put you in charge, man?" Bear waved the glowing tip at him.

"No one. But after what happened to our last publicist, someone here has to be smart or everything will go to shit. You want to make some money or what?"

"All right, all right." Bear pushed the joint into the ground. "I need to get some sleep, anyway, if we're doing a few sets later."

"I'll be back well before the first one. We can't stuff this up. There's too much riding on this festival. We've got to make up for what that fucking journalist wrote. I've a good mind to sue the paper."

Slim sat up and rubbed his eyes. "I'll watch out for Holly. Don't worry she's not into the hard stuff. Just a bit of weed. You go and do whatever it is you have to do." The tall, lanky guitarist pushed himself up from the ground in one lithe movement and followed David out of the tent. "So it was her?"

David nodded and stared across the field in the direction of their two cottages. "It was. I don't know how the hell she did it, but I have to get her back before she realises and freaks out."

"Or before you lose her," Slim said.

"I can't afford to lose her. Who knows where she'd end up? I shouldn't have left her but she fell asleep." David knew he'd said too much already, and he grabbed Slim's shoulder. "Thanks, mate. I know I can rely on you." He gave him a wave and headed back along the towpath to the river.

His first priority was to get Megan back through the time gate and convince her she'd been at the current Glastonbury Festival and she had dreamed the rest...or something.

Including the hot sex. That had been one huge mistake.

I shouldn't have touched her. But I couldn't help myself.

His chest was heavy with regret. It was easy to be sorry after the event. He'd sworn he would never get involved with a woman again.

He didn't do relationships, period. The way he lived his life, it was too hard.

158

Casual sex, yes. Heavy emotional stuff, no. But a connection had been forged between them the minute he'd tripped over her. It wasn't just her beauty that attracted him. Her face was transparent and she carried a sadness that tugged at his heart. A familiar feeling of wanting to protect overwhelmed him and he swore softly.

Christ, will I never learn?

Especially not with someone who was living next door to him, for fuck's sake. Someone who obviously had problems of her own. And someone who'd followed him through the stones. He rubbed his hand across his jaw, the stubble grazing his fingertips. He had to try to get her back to the cottage without her realising what had happened, and then he would cut all contact with her.

Once he'd gotten her back safely through the time gate, he'd come back here and stay here until the festival was over, and she went back to Australia. He knew it was the coward's way out, but there was no way he was putting himself in temptation's way again.

He groaned. He'd had no control over his response once she'd put her hands on him. For a moment he was tempted to leave, forget the festival, and go back to his island.

But he couldn't let the band down. Their fame and glory was ahead of them. He'd had his but he couldn't ruin the band's by changing today—by changing the past.

He pulled his thoughts to the present and looked ahead as he strode along the side of the narrow brook. No one else was around now that it was light and he finally approached the place where he'd left Megan fast asleep. He fought the anticipation curling in his stomach at seeing her again. Hopefully, she was awake and dressed.

But she was gone. No sign of her.

Fuck. He was sure he was in the right place.

Ten minutes later, he'd walked the path twice but there was no sign of her. He paused and looked down. The grass was flattened where he'd lain with her. He closed his eyes, fighting the fresh surge of desire that pumped through his blood.

Running his fingers through his hair in frustration, he walked back to the field where the main tent was set up.

The dawn light stole over Glastonbury Tor. They'd missed the perfect time for going through the gate, and now they'd have to go at midday. David slammed his fist onto his palm as he stood and turned slowly, searching the fields. A nagging fear settled in him and grew with each step he took.

I have to find her.

The early morning sunlight shone across the fields and the crowd had grown overnight. Small tents and tepees had sprung up all over the fields between the cottages and the stages. Throngs of people were massed around each of the performance areas and the air was alive with music and the appreciative calls of the festival goers.

Where the fuck did she go?

Maybe she'd tried to walk back home? Maybe she was in the crowd somewhere? If she did know about the gate, maybe she'd gone back through already?

Wherever she was he had to find her, and quickly. Making a snap decision and trying to forestall the worst thing that she could do, he turned to cross the field back to the cottages. If she wasn't there, he'd backtrack and come back to the festival. There was plenty of time before their ten o'clock set. If she'd gone back to the cottage and come across Alice McLaren, she'd think she was crazy. Maybe Jules's ghost story would come in handy after all.

The low murmur of voices drifted across to him, and the sweet smell of dope pervaded the morning air as the smells and the bright morning light filled him with a buzz. Blood pumped through his legs and his muscles tightened as he strode out. Megan's scent stayed with him and he could still feel her fingers

161

gripping his shoulders. He closed his eyes and took a few deep breaths before he set out for the cottage.

Forget her. Get her home safely and leave her alone.

Keeping to the edge of the field and staying well away from the stone markers, David reached the back gate of his cottage in less than thirty minutes. A wisp of smoke curled from the chimney at Violet Cottage and he groaned.

With any luck, she had come back and gone to bed and not noticed anything was different.

Who was he kidding? It was 1971 and Alice was in Violet Cottage.

The whole flaming garden was different and as he crossed the porch, the lack of roses and the back porch with no furniture stood out like a beacon.

Christ, all it needed was a sign saying "welcome to 1971" and it couldn't be more bleeding obvious that it was a different time.

David stepped to the door as the sound of a woman singing softly drifted out through the window.

He raised his hand to knock but the door opened before his fingers touched the wood.

"Holy shit." David closed his eyes and groaned.

Chapter Fourteen

Megan's stomach grumbled as the aroma of cooking meat wafted over to her. The second band to play after the Bowie cover had just finished its set and she hadn't heard of either of them. There must have been last-minute dropouts because none of the artists she'd been expecting to see had made an appearance. They must be playing later in the day. There was no sign of David and she bit her lip.

She had no idea what the deal was. Had he gotten what he'd been looking for the night before and now he'd taken off?

Stay here, Megan. I'm going to see the guys. Yeah, sure.

It might have been the most mind-blowing sex she'd ever had, but she was going to chalk that up to the music and the strange state she'd been in ever since she'd passed out in the field. After her Greg experience, she thought she'd learned her lesson. But one look at David and she'd lost control completely. *Damn it, what came over me?*

The only reason she was here was because she'd been worried about him when he'd disappeared behind the stone monument thing. And now, thanks to him, she had no shoes and no money.

David had told her to wait, but there was no way she was going to hang around for him to come back.

If he did.

She'd go back to the cottage, shower, change, grab her ticket and program, then get ready to listen to the bands and talk to music lovers in the crowd. She'd come over here to Glastonbury to work and she needed to get started.

Twisting around, she tried to get her bearings. She was sure she'd come across that field to the east but it was full of tents she hadn't noticed earlier.

"You look hungry, love. Want some soup?"

A young woman standing behind a wooden table in the tent behind her waved a large spoon in her direction.

"Sorry." She shook her head. "I haven't got my wallet with me."

The woman leaned forward, her long braids dangling over her shoulders down to her waist. She held on to a small child with one hand and pointed to a sign at the front of the table with the other. FREE was emblazoned in large block letters.

"Love food here, free for all comers."

"Free?" Megan sniffed appreciatively and looked over to the large pot bubbling on a gas ring at the back of the open-sided tent.

"Soup, mulled wine…and hash cookies. All in the name of peace and love." The woman picked the child up and hoisted him onto her hip. "You give to the universe, you get back. Want some?"

Megan nodded and watched as the woman balanced the child on her hip while she ladled steaming vegetables and broth into a paper mug for her. "Do you do this at many festivals?"

"We came to the first festival last year, but because the villagers were so against us 'hippies' going to the cafés in the village, we decided to help out this year."

Megan narrowed her eyes. "What do you mean the first one?"

"The first Glastonbury. Last year at the Worthy Farm they gave free milk, so we wanted to do our bit this year. Give and the universe gives back to you."

"Last year?" She had no idea what the woman was talking about. She'd studied the Glastonbury phenomenon and it had run every year since 1978 after the first couple of festivals in 1970 and 1971. Since then it had been big business.

But this festival was nowhere like the commercial one she'd expected. A shiver ran down Megan's back

165

as a strange thought entered her mind. She rubbed her arms to dispel the goose bumps.

It's almost as though I'm at one of the early festivals. It's like a re-creation.

Megan looked down at her bare feet. "Can you point me in the direction of the village?" On the way back to the cottage, she'd call in at the little store and buy a pair of flip-flops and put them on the tab. And while she was there, she'd see if the library had Wi-Fi. She hadn't thought of that the other day—and she had a feeling David had only taken her to Taunton as part of the get-to-know-me-I'm-a-nice-guy routine so he could get in her pants. Well, he had, but no more.

The woman stepped out from behind the table and led Megan to the other side of the wide pathway between the tents. "If you follow this path to the end of the big tents and then go through the stile, you'll come to the road that goes to the village."

Megan thanked the woman and headed down past the tents, sipping on the soup as she strolled through the crowd. The morning sun was warm and there were people lying on the grass sunbathing. A few called out a friendly greeting as she walked past and her fingers itched to start taking notes. The opportunity for research was amazing and everyone was happy and relaxed. She couldn't believe the number of women with no tops on, breasts bared to the sun. A couple of

166

the guys she passed had nothing on at all, and their white English skin was starting to burn. It was surreal; the seventies feel was all around her. Maybe it was just that England was old-fashioned and different from Australia? She shook her head as that frisson of uncertainty ran down her spine again. Music blared across the fields from the performance tents but she didn't recognise any of the bands or songs. She kept her eyes peeled for David and his mates but there was no sign of any of them.

She threw the paper cup into a bin next to the stile and climbed through. As the woman had said there would be, a path led from the stile to a narrow road where a sign on the grass pointed the way to Glastonbury.

With a yawn, Megan set off for the village, keeping to the grass beneath the hedgerows to protect her bare feet.

Chapter Fifteen

"Davy? You're back." The woman opened the door wide and smiled until she looked at him. "What's wrong?"

"Hello, Alice." David's breath hitched. He'd run the whole way across the field to the cottages, giving the stones a wide berth. "I've lost someone."

Alice McLaren wiped her hands on a bright floral apron and held her arms out to him. "I'm surprised to see you. I thought you'd be immersed in the festival."

David reached over and hugged her. Alice had grown her hair since he'd last seen her and she kept hold of his hands and looked at him. "Still looking good, Davy." She tipped her head to the side. "You don't change?"

"I know. I don't understand it myself." All he knew was, he stayed the same age whichever time he was in. "You've had no unexpected visitors this morning?"

"No. I haven't seen anyone. What's happened?"

David ran his fingers through his hair as he stood at the door. This was doing his head in.

"I've lost someone… a friend…a woman. It's a long story and if I don't find her, she won't be able to find her way back." He took another deep breath.

"Stay there, I'll get you a cool drink. You look like you need it."

When Alice returned, he took the tumbler of water gratefully. Closing his eyes, he drank deeply to soothe his parched throat. "Thanks."

"I'm pleased to hear you have another friend."

"It's hard, Alice, so I spend most of my time in the twenty-first century when I'm not on tour with the band.

"Only the twenty-first century?" Alice stared at him, a frown marring her face. "You haven't been exploring other times, have you? I warned you about that."

"No, I listened to you." David took another gulp. "Alice, apart from loving my music and performing, I hate the whole seventies scene. The drugs, the— pardon me, free sex—the groupies. The whole lack of privacy thing. And then dealing with Emma's death while she was in our employ…" He stared out the window. "You know what a mess I was last year and I'll be forever grateful to you for helping me get through it. It suits me very well to live in the twenty-first century. I get the best of both times without being a part of that ghastly scene, and I don't want to put my privacy in jeopardy."

The morning light shimmered in the distance and a quiver of unease shot through him.

"I arrived in 2008, and I stayed there. The only time I come back to the seventies is to tour occasionally and to record with the band. That does my head in enough."

"David, you must—"

He held up his hand as he interrupted her. "Sorry to be rude, but I have to get back to the festival and find Megan. If she discovers what's happened to her, she'll freak out. And I don't want her to find out she's gone back in time."

"Listen to me." Alice caught his hand between hers. "You have to stop taking responsibility for everyone. People make their own choices and you can't protect everyone."

"You are a wise lady, but I don't think so, not in this case." He leaned down and kissed her cheek and was immediately cocooned in the heady fragrance of sandalwood oil. "Now I have to go."

Alice looked at him curiously. "Am I still around in 2008?"

"Yes, and you are the sweetest old lady." David looked at her with a smile as he handed her the glass. "I have to go and find Megan."

"Be happy, David."

He set out across the field as the door closed softly behind him At least he didn't have to tell Alice that 2008 was the year she'd passed away, and now three years later, the woman he was looking for was staying in her cottage.

***

Despite feeling a little bit lost, Megan fought the uncertainty tugging at her. She smiled as she strolled along the edge of the road in the softly dappled shade of the hedgerows and she took a deep breath of the fresh, clean air. The sweet twittering of tiny birds as they flitted in and out of the tangled vines gradually replaced the sound of the music fading behind her and calm filled her. The soft morning light and the gentle music of the birds were so different to home. Even in the city amid the traffic noises, the raucous sounds of kookaburras and crows filled the air around her apartment. As she thought of home, the calm disappeared and a sudden knot formed in her stomach. She really needed to get in touch with Tony and find out if he had made any progress in incriminating Greg, or there would be no point to all her research at the festival. If they threw her out of her job, it would apply to her doctoral study too.

Breathing deeply, she blocked the thoughts from her mind and concentrated on enjoying the walk to the village. Her visit to the festival was far from what she'd anticipated—including the tryst with David last night.

Turning into the main street, she crossed the village green to the shop and was taken aback to see a large sign in the window.

Bold black block letters proclaimed, HIPPIES NOT WELCOME.

Strange. Not a term used for the Generation Xers and Yers of the twenty-first century. Not in Australia, anyway. The bucolic countryside of rural England was certainly still living in the past. And it was just what David had told her about the seventies festivals.

No, it was impossible.

If it was a dream, it was the longest, strangest dream she'd ever had.

More material for my thesis. She needed to get back to the cottage and get some of this down before she forgot half of it. Yawning, she rubbed her eyes. Her mind was still fuzzy around the edges and she needed to take a quick nap before she returned to the festival.

The bell on the door tinkled as she pushed it open and entered the dark shop.

"We haven't got none." A sharp voice came from behind the counter. Megan looked around to see who the woman was speaking to, but as far as she could see, she was the only customer in the shop.

A shopkeeper stood with her arms folded and a frown wrinkling her forehead.

"Ah, do you have any shoes here?" Megan pointed down to her bare feet. "Just a pair of rubber thongs—I mean flip-flops—will do."

"No." The woman scowled at her. "Go back to your hippie friends and share theirs. I don't sell any."

"There's some up there. Just a medium-size pair, please." Megan pointed to the shelf of flip-flops high above the woman's head. "Oh, and I'll have to put them on the McLaren cottage tab, please. Jules said to do that yesterday."

"No tabs here, so I can't sell you nothing."

"But Jules said yesterday—"

"There ain't no Jules works here." The woman came from behind the counter and crossed to the door. "I'm closing for elevenses now so you'll have to go." Opening the door, she stood with her foot wedged against the bottom and stared at Megan.

Confused, Megan walked to the door. It was nowhere near eleven o'clock. Her gaze fell on the newspaper rack along the window. She leaned forward and picked up the *Taunton Times* and froze, ignoring the woman's protests in the background.

"Put it down. I told you there's no credit here."

Megan caught her breath as the room spun. She reached for the door and held on with one hand as she scanned the newspaper. The lurid headline in bold black letters proclaimed *Davy Morgan Drug Scandal. He Was With Her When She Died,* and as she dropped her eyes to the other articles, disbelief crawled icily through her veins. On the bottom of the page was an article saying John Lennon had just gone into the Abbey Road Studios in London to record his new album called *Imagine.* Squinting in the dim interior she struggled to read the date at the top of the paper. She looked around at the shop. Maybe they were selling retro stuff to go with the festival? She was grasping at straws.

Maybe my suspicions are right, after all.

"What's the date?" she demanded, turning to the unpleasant shopkeeper.

The woman shrank back as Megan's voice rose, and she dropped the hand she'd held out for the newspaper. "It's the 26th June."

"What year?"

"What?"

Megan closed her eyes and dropped the newspaper onto the floor beside her as the woman stared at her.

"That's why we don't let hippies into the village. You've addled your brains with all that pot smoking and sex." The woman almost spat the words at Megan as she bent to pick up the crumpled newspaper. "Now get out of my shop and don't come back. You and your type aren't welcome here."

Megan opened her eyes and the room had stopped spinning. "Please, just tell me what year it is?" Her voice shook as she whispered softly.

The woman must have taken some pity on her and she answered gruffly, "It's 1971, of course."

***

David kept close to the low stone wall and gave the markers a wide berth as he crossed the fields back to Worthy Farm. The air was still and almost shimmering with expectation. Going through the time gates was always quickest at this time of day and especially during the solstice. Once, he'd slipped through accidentally without even lining the markers up. That was the last thing he needed today—to go back unintentionally and leave Megan here.

He took a deep breath to dispel the unease that had settled in his chest since he'd returned to the brook to find her missing. As he turned to cross the last field,

175

the sound of a small truck travelling towards the village reached him. Glancing across, he paused and put his hand on the sun-warmed fence. It might be worth cutting across to the village; maybe she'd left the festival and decided to go back to the cottage through Glastonbury. Bracing himself on one hand, he climbed over the waist-high fence and turned east towards the buildings across the wide green field.

The main street was quiet and the store was closed. An elderly man digging in his garden scowled at him and turned away as he crossed to the pub.

The publican was at the side of the building rolling a keg of beer around to the side door. "Hey, Ken." David called a greeting to the burly man.

Ken straightened and wiped his hands on his jeans before reaching his hand out to shake David's hand.

"Davy, boy! Good to see you." He pumped David's hand vigorously. "What brings you into the village so early?"

"What time is it, Ken?" He'd gotten to know Ken last year when he'd stayed at the pub with Emma when he'd come down from London. He'd brought her here to try to get her away from the fast crowd she'd been hanging with. He'd be forever grateful that Bear and Slim were having a drink there that lazy Sunday afternoon. They'd hooked up and Davy had joined them as lead singer of their band. Ken was good friends with Arabella Churchill, who was the main organiser of the festival, and he was one of the few villagers who welcomed the musicians and visitors. He'd told David about the vacant cottage next to Alice when he'd been looking for somewhere else to live.

"Almost nine. I thought you'd be sleeping in after that great performance the band put on last night. Great show, man."

"Shit, I have to be back for our next set at ten." David ran his hand through his hair in frustration. He'd lost track of the time in his concern for Megan. "I'm looking for a girl…a woman."

"Who?" Ken winked at him. "Plenty over at the Worthy Farm."

"A tall woman. Dark reddish hair. Red jeans, black T-shirt."

Ken's face lit up in a grin. "You're in luck, Davy. Old Mrs. Carmichael just gave her short shrift at the village store and slammed the shop door behind her when she left. The old biddy was the first one to put the no hippies sign up."

"Where did she go?" Relief coursed through David's chest as he looked around.

"She headed down the high street towards the cottages. You've only just missed her. She went around the corner as I got the keg off the truck."

"Thank you." David ran down the street in the direction Ken pointed, his breath hitching by the time he got to the corner.

Megan was walking slowly along the edge of the road only a couple of hundred yards ahead of him.

"Megan!"

She lifted her head as his call reached her and stepped into the shadow of the hedgerow, waiting as he closed the distance between them.

His feelings were in conflict as he ran towards her. The relief at finding her safe in this time warred with a surging excitement. His body still hummed from the experience with her last night. Never in his life had he been filled with such pure joy when he'd been with a woman. It rivalled the emotion he got from his music and that frightened him. He let his gaze wander over her, from the line of her shoulders down her back where her auburn hair hung like a silk curtain.

"God, Megan. Where did you go?" He gently took her by the shoulders and stared down at her, before pulling her against him, warmth surging though his body as her skin touched his. Her dark eyes were hooded and her mouth was set in a straight line. He'd been going to kiss her lips but he dropped his head and kissed her cheek instead as she stood rigid in his arms.

She stiffened in his grasp. "Why didn't you come back? I thought you'd left me."

David stepped back and held her gaze. Her face was pale and there were dark shadows beneath her eyes. "I got held up. I'm just so happy to see you safe."

"Why wouldn't I be safe?" She looked at him with a strange expression on her face. "I gave up waiting for you and now I'm heading to the cottage to have a shower and get my stuff. It was the craziest night and the morning's not been much better."

"You can't." He racked his brain for a good reason to convince her to come back with him, because crossing the time gate right now was not a good idea. But he drew a blank.

"What? I want to go home, have a shower, and take a nap before I come back to the festival." Megan pulled away from him. "There is so much material, I have to come back and do some interviews."

"You can't."

"I can't what?"

"You can't go back yet. You have to come with me."

"Like hell. Who do you think you are to tell me what to do?" She turned around and strode down the road in the direction of the cottages. "Just because of

179

what happened between us last night gives you no right to boss me around."

He had to think of a way to get her to come with him. He wasn't going to be responsible for putting her in danger. He ran his fingers through his hair.

But that's the least of my problems. He had to find a way to get her to the time gate without telling her what was going on.

Striding behind her, he caught up to her and grabbed her arm. She jerked away angrily.

"Leave me alone."

"That's not the message I got from you last night."

She glared at him. "Yeah, well, last night was last night and this is today."

"Look, it's still about three miles this way to the cottage. Come back with me."

Megan frowned at him and bit her lip. He could almost hear her thoughts. She was totally pissed off with him. "Look, we had sex. It was great. But you left me and *now* you're trying to tell me I have to come back with you?" She looked down at her bare feet and he waited for her to make a decision. "Give me one good reason why I should."

"I'll borrow Bear's van and drive you home as soon as we finish our set. You can listen to the band again and you won't have to walk back in your bare feet."

If that didn't work and she decided to keep going, he was going to have to force her to go with him, and he didn't want to have to do that, especially since he couldn't think of any way to do that, apart from putting her over his shoulder.

"All right," she said begrudgingly and he let out the breath he'd been holding. "I suppose that makes sense and I get to hear your band play again." Finally, she flashed him a strange smile. "You do a brilliant cover version of your *uncle's* music. I'd really like to interview you about why you only play *his* songs."

"We'll talk about that later. I need to get back. We're on stage at ten."

She stared at him with that strange smile on her face.

"What's wrong?" he said.

"I'm really interested to hear what you have to say about your music, and *his* music."

"Of course," he agreed.

Anything to get her to stay with me. I have to keep her safe.

She was putting out strange vibes and for a moment, it was almost as though she knew where— or rather when— they were. He held out his hand but she ignored it, and he shrugged.

"Come on, we'll cut across the field behind the village. It's the shortest way back to Worthy Farm."

181

"The Worthy Farm? I thought the festival was at Pilton Farm?" Her eyes narrowed and for a moment he was unsure how to answer her.

"Yeah, you're right. Got my farms mixed up. Come on, I'll miss the set." He turned away from her, willing her silently to follow him, but not game to turn around and check that she was. David turned and strode ahead, and was relieved when she caught up to him. He had less than an hour to get back, get her safely ensconced on the side of the stage where he was not going to take his eyes off her. Then he'd figure out what to tell her about going back through the gate.

Thank God it was only a short set this morning.

Chapter Sixteen

Megan hurried to keep up with David when he came to a turnstile in the fence. He stepped back and waited for her to climb through first.

"Thank you." She nodded. Her thoughts were still whirling around. Even though she'd been angry at him for trying to boss her around, she had been relieved to see him when he appeared behind her on the way to the cottage. Her mind was still foggy, as though it was full of cotton wool, and she wasn't sure what was real or whether she was dreaming.

When she'd picked up the paper in the village store, she'd recognised it straight away. It was the same article she'd been reading on her laptop on the plane and now she intended to read it again as soon as she got back to the cottage. Did the strange woman in the shop really say it was 1971 or had she imagined that? Did she really go into the village shop or was that a dream? Did everyone really look and act as though it was the seventies?

Are they all crazy, or am I?

As they walked along the field, a bright and shiny red Mustang roared along the road at the edge of the field. The traffic was building as the festival got going. Megan stopped and put her hands on her hips as three VW Kombi vans trundled past, their engines revving as they drove up the slight hill.

Everything was confirming her suspicions. Truth was, she'd been terrified to go back to the cottage by herself. Not knowing what she was going to find there.

It was bizarre. The more she thought about it, the more everything pointed to her being in a different time, in the same place.

The clothes, the music, the small crowd at the festival and the way they were behaving. The different woman in the shop today and that newspaper headline. The clothes they were wearing. It was all so…so seventies.

Either she was dreaming or she'd taken leave of her senses. Maybe she'd had a breakdown because of the news about her job. Add in some jet lag and who knows…? A cold prickly feeling crept up her chest and her breath caught. She stopped and put her hand to her head as it all overwhelmed her.

Where the hell did David fit into the whole mess? Until she knew, she wasn't going to say anything to him. Because if she was right, he wasn't David. He *was* Davy Morgan. The real Davy Morgan.

"What's wrong?" His voice was kind and a shiver ran down her back at the same time warmth pooled between her thighs. She wasn't used to a guy worrying about her…but it was…sort of okay. Despite the confusion of her thoughts, her body pulled towards him, craving physical closeness. She fought the desire to lean into him and let him hold her.

"Nothing." She held her hand to her head. "I have a slight headache. I need to sleep, and have a drink. Maybe I'm dehydrated?"

He reached up and gently pushed her hair back from her face. She couldn't help turning into his hand. "I did get some sleep after you left, but it was a pretty exhausting way we spent the night." Her heartbeat increased as she remembered the feel of him moving inside her. It had been the most amazing sexual experience of her life.

"You're all flushed. I'll get you some food and something cold to drink while we play and then I'll get you back home as soon as we're finished. It's a really short set. We're just introducing—" He broke off and didn't finish the sentence.

"Introducing who, David?"

185

He looked away across the field and wouldn't meet her eye.

"Just a new band. You'll see."

The crowd had gotten even bigger in the time she'd been in the village and Kombi vans lined the narrow lane beside the fence.

Megan looked up at David, deciding to fish a little bit without giving away her suspicions. "There are a lot of old VWs here."

"Yeah." He cleared his throat. "It's a free festival and a lot of people who can't afford the big gigs come down from the city in their beat-up old cars." He didn't sound convincing and she pushed on with her questions.

"So how come the old cars are so bright and shiny?" Then she realised what he'd said.

"What do you mean a free festival? I had to pay a heap for my three-day ticket."

"Errr…I must have misunderstood. I assumed it was free." He wouldn't meet her eye and Megan knew he was lying. "I'm only a simple musician. I'm not sure what's going on. Come on, the guys are going to be worried." The more that was said, the more her certainty grew that somehow, she was at the 1971 festival and he was trying to hide it from her. She shook her head. Now she was thinking crazy thoughts too.

Maybe that soup had something in it?

He grabbed her hand and dragged her through the crowd. Warmth shot up her arm and she resisted the urge to curl her fingers in his. She had no idea what was going on, who he really was, or *when* she was.

Bloody hell, I can't concentrate.

David Morgan was a mass of contradictions. The man who was pulling her along behind him and expressing such concern for her well-being was poles apart from the rude guy who'd greeted her the other night, and very different again from the man who had taken her to heaven and back again last night. Now he was looking after her. Taking a breath and shaking her head, she tried to clear it and stay focused on the present.

Whenever that was.

"So why is everyone dressed in seventies clothes?"

"I don't know, Megan. Like I said, I'm just a musician. I'm not the fount of all knowledge about the festival. You're the sociologist."

"Don't worry. I intend to find out everything I can. Trust me. I am *very* interested in what's happening around me." She pulled her hand from his as he stopped at the back of the pyramid stage. A set of stairs led to the stage about ten feet above them and

187

David stood back and gestured for her to climb up. She hesitated.

"Come on, I don't want to lose you again." He put his hands on her waist and lifted her onto the first step, and her skin burned where his fingers gripped her firmly.

"You can sit on the side of the stage and you'll have the best seat in the house." He stood in front of her and his eyes were level with hers. His face was so close, his breath fanned her hot cheeks and she looked down as she felt it stirring along her skin. She didn't move, and continued to watch him. And wait.

Will I never learn? Focus.

Finally, she turned away and grabbed the rope that ran up each side of the stairs, conscious of him close behind her.

"Thank God, man." The two men she'd met at the pub yesterday, his band members, Bear and Slim, stood at the edge of the suspended wooden platform. As she looked up at them, she remembered how she knew their names. Bear and Slim were the nicknames of the two guys in Davy Morgan's band. She'd read it in that article on her laptop. On the CDs she'd listened to for years, they were credited under their real names, but it was only yesterday in that article about a scandal involving Davy that she'd read their nicknames

Holy shit. It is1971. How the hell had that happened? She racked her brain, reliving every moment of the past few hours. It had all turned crazy after she'd woken up in the first aid tent. After she'd followed David through the field after he'd disappeared.

And I touched that stone. That was it.

It was like something out of a bloody historical novel. Time travel? No way?

She shook her head, on the brink of tears.

"We thought you weren't going to get back in time," Bear said as he nodded at Megan. "He found you okay, I see?"

David nodded without speaking as he slid a small wooden chair behind the brown hessian covering that was hanging at the side of the stage. When he had pushed it into the shadows, he turned to her and once again his strong fingers gripped her waist as he lifted her and put her in the chair. Megan sat and watched, bemused as he turned to Slim and finally spoke.

"Have you got anything to drink? Any food?"

From behind Bear's drums, Slim retrieved a backpack and dug inside and pulled out a glass bottle.

David frowned as his fingers circled the neck of the narrow glass bottle and passed it to Megan. "At least Coke will give you some energy."

She took the cold glass bottle from him, holding it up in front of her.

"Hmm, one of those retro Coke bottles?" She watched as the two men exchanged a glance.

"Yeah, a retro bottle."

Ha! Sure it is.

The floor creaked as another man jumped up from the top step onto the stage.

"No groupies allowed up here, Davy." The older guy was dressed in a business suit and he pointed across at Megan.

"No problem. She's my girlfriend, and she wasn't feeling well. I want to keep an eye on her while we do our set." David reached for his guitar and slung the strap over his shoulder.

"Fair enough." After flicking a disinterested glance at Megan, he went to the edge of the stage. "Fabulous crowd. A lot more than we'd hoped for. The first festival was an impromptu one but we've trebled the crowd this year.

"Ready? It's only a minute till you're on." The guy looked at his watch. "Where's Holly?"

David shook his head, "Haven't seen her since she was asleep in the tent. Maybe she's still down there." Megan was surprised to see a frown cross his face, and she narrowed her eyes.

Who's Holly? A girlfriend?

"Slim, is she okay? Can you go down and check on her?"

"You haven't got time. I'll go down and look for her while you're playing. Okay?" The man shot David a sympathetic look and Megan wondered what was going on.

"Thanks, Brian."

David stepped to the front, but seemed to stay back far enough to keep Megan in his line of sight. Slim walked across and flicked the switches on two large amplifiers next to the speakers and a loud buzz filled the stage. A roar came up from the crowd below and then it hushed with anticipation. Bear slid in behind the drums on the slightly raised platform in the centre of the large stage and grinned at Megan as he stretched and raised his arms above his head.

The energy on the stage was palpable as Brian walked past David.

Megan's head spun with excitement as the hum from the amplifiers surrounded her, and she lifted the cool glass bottle and held it against her cheek, conscious of David's gaze fixed on her even as his fingers slid gracefully along the neck of the guitar. A shiver ran down her back and it was more from the intense expression on his face than the cold glass against her skin.

"Music lovers of Glastonbury 1971, let's enjoy Davy Morgan and his band." The voice of the announcer boomed over the microphone followed by loud drumming as Bear crashed his drumsticks down. Then there was silence.

Megan closed her eyes as a roar came from the crowd below and the plaintive notes of one of her favourite Davy Morgan songs hung in the air.

Music lovers of Glastonbury 1971!

He had said 1971. Nineteen seventy-one. Bloody hell.

Either she was dreaming or crazy, or something in this place had taken her back in time. If this was 1971, then David really was *Davy* Morgan. It was too much to take in. She closed her eyes and let the music fill her—she'd worry later and figure out what to do. In the meantime, she would make the most of wherever—or *whenever*—she was.

The beat of the music hollowed out and Davy started to sing.

Because it was Davy Morgan's voice. The voice she'd listened to for so long.

The lyrics were filled with sadness and longing and Megan kept her eyes tightly closed and sang the words, her lips moving slowly in time with the beat and the long-held notes.

My love is for you

Time doesn't matter
It holds no meaning.

The chorus began and the crowd joined in and the mass of voices rose from below.

Free as a bird to come and leave on the air
Through time, through time.

The words she knew so well had a completely new meaning for her now. Megan kept her eyes squeezed shut. She didn't open them because she knew David's gaze was still on her. The feeling warmed her skin as if he'd placed his fingers on her. She knew he watched her as he sang. She held her breath as the music built to a final crescendo, and the long, lonely guitar riff that heralded the last verse filled her ears. The music flowed through her skin, filled her mind and her soul. Her limbs were weightless and she imagined she was flying like the bird in Davy's song. It was the same feeling she'd experienced last night when Davy had lain with her at the side of the small brook.

For fifteen minutes, she sat with her head back and her eyes closed, as the music swirled around her. Warmth flowed through her and the same sexual excitement that had ripped through her nerve endings last night gripped her once again. Opening her eyes, she lifted her gaze to Davy and the sexual energy crackled between them. His dark brooding eyes were fixed on her and she knew he felt the same desire she did. Her lips parted softly and she ran her hands slowly up her arms as she held his gaze.

***

As soon as the first word had left his lips, and Megan had closed her eyes, David was enthralled. The synergy of the band flowed and completed the circle they always strove for, but this time, Megan was a part of it. She leaned back in the chair with her eyes closed and when her mouth moved with the song, all David could think of was the feel of her lips beneath his.

As the blood surged to his groin and he swelled with wanting her, he was grateful for the long loose shirt that hung over his jeans, because the whole audience would have witnessed what he was feeling.

Music always filled him with desire and restlessness, but he'd never before experienced this connection with a woman. God, there'd been plenty of girls available whenever he'd needed to lose himself after performing—even back in the early days when he had played the pubs by himself. Over the years, the excitement of hooking up with different girls had paled, and it had bored him. There had been no feeling in it. For him, it was a quick coupling to assuage a basic need; for the girls it was simply the opportunity to say they'd slept with Davy Morgan.

And when they found out which hotel the band was staying at, they wouldn't leave him alone. That's why finding the cottage next door to Alice had been a godsend.

David played without being conscious of the notes that came from his guitar and the words that fell from his lips. He thought back over the events that had led to his living across two centuries. Right up until yesterday when Megan had followed him through the time slip, he'd kidded himself that he had it all thought out and had been confident he could make music in one time and live his life privately in another. He knew the risk of changing anything in the past. Writing and playing his music were no threat, he rationalised to himself, but now another person was involved and it had become fraught with danger.

When the drums crashed loudly and Slim used the pedal to wind down the last sad notes of the final song of their set, Megan was staring at him and Davy's world came crashing down as he fell into her eyes.

Those beautiful eyes. The hunger in them echoes how I feel. How the hell am I going to keep my hands off her?

Oblivious to the screams of the crowd and the others on the stage around them, he slid his guitar from his shoulder and walked over to her.

I can't. Relief flooded through him as he let his need consume him.

He held out his hand without breaking their gaze and her hand gripped his as he pulled her from the chair. Her body was soft against his, her breasts moulded by the thin T-shirt she wore. Her arms went around his neck and he lowered his lips and claimed her mouth.

It didn't matter when he was, he'd found where he wanted to be.

***

"Ken's got a room." The deep voice filled with mirth gradually intruded on Megan's senses. Her world had whirled around her once David's hot mouth had taken hers in a savage kiss. She hadn't cared where she was or who else was around. All she needed was the touch of David against her. If this was a different world, and a different time she'd somehow fallen into, so be it. If it felt like this, she was happy to stay here.

As long as it was real. She would die if she woke up and it was all a dream.

Gradually, movement on the stage brought her back to reality. At the same time, David pulled his lips away but he kept one arm tightly around her. She needed it; her body was still screaming for his touch.

196

"Bear, can I borrow your van?" His deep voice sent a shiver down her back.

"Sure, don't need it for a while. Slim and I are going to have a wander round and chill out for a while." Bear winked at her. "We're not on again till tomorrow afternoon so you two lovebirds have a whole day and a night."

David pulled away from her slightly and Megan's legs trembled as his hand stopped supporting her. But he was only gone for a second as he reached for his guitar. As he picked it up his arm came firmly around her back again.

"Thanks, Bear. And can you make sure Holly is okay?" He lowered his voice and turned to his band mates, who stood at the side of the stage. "In case I don't make it back, I'll park the van on the other side of the village. About a mile down."

Bear and Slim came over together and each shook Davy's free hand.

"Try your best, man. Our music needs you." Slim turned to Megan. "Make sure he comes back, won't you, dolls?"

Megan looked from one to the other and though she sensed that something had changed she couldn't understand what. Nodding, she held her hand out and Bear squeezed it.

"I certainly will. The world needs Davy Morgan and his music."

She felt David tense beside her as his arm gripped her tightly. She looked up at him and smiled.

"You don't have to tell me where I am. Or rather, *when* I am." She lifted her hand and held it against his lips. "I know."

Chapter Seventeen

Bear's van was parked a long way from the back of the stage. As they walked through the crowd, David kept his head down but it still wasn't enough to keep fans from stopping him. The guitar on his shoulder was a dead giveaway.

"Can I have your autograph please?" David glanced down at Megan as the girl in front of him passed him a pen and lifted her shirt, baring her breasts. He grinned and dashed an autograph on the top of the girl's arm.

Megan chuckled as they walked away from her to the van. "So, the job has some perks then? It's not just playing music?"

"You could say that. But it's not all it's cracked up to be." David opened the van door and reached beneath the seat and pulled out the keys. He led Megan around to the other side and opened the door. "I'll tell you all about it later."

When he got in the driver's seat, he looked into the back of the small van and turned to Megan to apologise. Before he could speak, she leaned over the narrow space between them and caught his chin with her hand and kissed him.

"Do you know what you do to me? How you make me feel?" Her eyes were heavy-lidded and her soft breath warmed his cheek as she spoke. "I feel this incredible connection with you." She pulled back and looked up at him with a frown wrinkling her forehead. "I don't know if it has something to do with what's happened to me…to us…" She shook her head. "But I've never experienced anything like it before. When you're near me, I need to feel you touching me."

She moved across and wound her arms around his neck and moaned softly as his mouth took hers.

God help me, I can't get enough of her. He deepened the kiss and her tongue danced with his. The blood hummed through his body and he fought to keep control.

Gently he pulled back, and took her arms from around his neck and held her hands between his.

"I need to feel your hands on me." She took his hand and laid it on her thigh, and David groaned as her thigh muscle tightened beneath his fingers.

David lifted his hand and held her gaze. Her lips were parted, and she stared with uninhibited desire at

200

him. It was one of the hardest things he'd done, but he tore his eyes away and looked out onto the street to get his control back. He took a deep breath and crossed his arms.

Before I rip her clothes off right here in this grotty van.

"I know exactly what you're saying. I understand how you feel. This time stuff can screw with your head." He chose his words deliberately to try to put some distance between them, to move away from the sexual tension that was hovering around them. "I'll explain everything to you when we get you back to the cottage. Or as much as I can, anyway."

Megan glanced into the back of the van. A mattress butted against the bare metal walls and it was covered with food wrappers and empty bottles. A pile of clothes held an indentation the shape of a head, and had obviously been used as a pillow.

"So we don't have time…" She glanced back at the mattress.

David's blood heated as he saw the naked hunger on her face. It was the most beautiful thing he'd ever seen.

She wants me as much as I need her.

"No, not here." He laughed as he looked back at the mess in the back of the van. "The first time I laid with you was under the stars with the sound of water playing music to us. The second is *not* going to be in Bear's van." He couldn't do it. Her body was calling to be touched and he leaned in and kissed her, running his finger down the front of her T-shirt and cradling her breast in his palm. "No matter how much I need to."

"This is really out of character for me. The intensity is, well…it's just peculiar." Megan's voice was husky. "I don't do this."

"It's okay. Just chill," he reassured her. "It will be interesting to see if these feelings stay when we go back…it's almost like a craving…an addiction."

A flicker of uncertainty ran over Megan's face. "Tell me what's going to happen."

"We drive to the field where the stones are and I'll find the time gate on the ley line. We need to get there by midday."

"To where?"

"The stones." David let Megan's hand go and the loss that shot through his body rocked him to the core. His hand went out to hold her again and he wasn't aware of the action. He grabbed hold of the steering wheel and looked ahead. It had to be something to do with the time shift; he was becoming more certain of that every time he touched Megan, and it worried him.

Whatever it was, it seemed to have the same effect on her. Although if he was honest, he'd been attracted to her since he'd landed on top of her on the porch.

"I'll explain it all soon."

***

Megan shivered as David let her hand go. While he was holding her or touching her, she felt grounded. She sighed with relief as he reached out and took her hand again.

Safe.

Even with the pure sexual desire that coursed through her every time he came near her or held her gaze, she trusted him implicitly. This connection between them seemed like something out of this world.

Eerie. Supernatural.

It was as though she'd been bewitched. Her life in Sydney seemed detached from the present and she had to concentrate really hard to grasp and hold the memory of anything before she'd woken up in that first aid tent yesterday. It was like being in a parallel universe, like something she watched at the movies. But she was in it. She didn't care about anything—or anyone she'd left behind there.

I'm totally out of my realm…

Fear knotted in her chest and Megan crossed her arms tightly in front of her as David started the car.

What was the present?

Confusion filled her thoughts. So much had happened in the last couple of days and they hadn't really talked about it. David had not admitted in so many words that he was actually Davy Morgan. Nor had he confirmed that she had gone back in time.

All he'd said was they had to go back to the stones.

As they drove through the village, she turned to look out the window as the village went by. She paid extra attention to the buildings and tried to remember what they had looked like when she'd walked to the pub for lunch the other day.

The only difference she could really see was the signs in the café and the village store saying HIPPIES NOT WELCOME. She hadn't noticed enough yesterday. The crazy old woman in the store talking about magnetics, solstices, and water had taken all of her attention. Reaching for the window winder inside the door, she gripped it tightly and it creaked as she wound down the window and the sweet fragrance of honeysuckle drifted in. Megan looked across the narrow street as David drove the old van slowly past the pub. The village looked as quaint as it had the other day. Geese dotted the green, and the whitewashed walls of the pub contrasted with the soft blue of the sky.

An idyllic scene, but sinister. The uncertainty of what lay ahead of her filled her veins with an icy fear and she fought the panic that rose in her chest. Unfolding her arms, she reached out and placed her hand on David's thigh, and immediately a calm stole over her, and the fear disappeared as quickly as it had come.

"I feel safe when I touch you." She looked across at him. His skin was fair, with a flush on his high cheekbones, and contrasted with the black curls tumbling past his face. "The fear disappears." As she watched he briefly closed his eyes and placed his hand on top of hers.

"And when *you* touch me, I feel decidedly unsafe."

"What do you mean?"

His gaze dropped to his jeans and heat rose from her chest to her neck. Not to mention the heat between her thighs.

"Right, you need to do some explaining. Forget about this feeling we seem to create whenever we're around each other." She changed the subject to get her thoughts away from pulling him into the back of the van and taking her clothes off. "Tell me exactly what's going on."

David glanced over at her before he pulled the van onto the side of the road, steering with one hand as he kept his hand on hers on his thigh. His dark lashes fanned his eyes and she couldn't see his expression. His lips were tight and his brow was wrinkled.

"Don't you dare close up on me, David…or Davy? You are Davy Morgan, aren't you? As crazy as it seems I know it's true." Megan snatched her hand from beneath his and tried to ignore the fear that crept back through her when she moved away from his touch.

David took the keys from the ignition and put them on the floor beneath the seat before he reached over and picked up his guitar. Without looking at her or speaking, he opened the car door and came around to her side and opened her door. The guitar was slung over his shoulder and he held his free hand out to her.

Megan looked up at him as she took his hand. "Well?"

"Come on, I'll tell you everything as we walk." He inclined his head towards the field on their left. Low bushy trees blocked her view past the field. "We have to cross two fields to get to the markers."

He tugged her hand and they set off through the gate in the fence. The grass was soft and cool beneath Megan's bare feet. A couple of black-and-white cows stood silently and watched them as they crossed to the middle of the field.

"I didn't know how much to tell you because this has never happened to me before." David's voice was low and Megan leaned closer as he continued. "I've always gone through the stones deliberately. Tell me what happened to you yesterday. When I left, you were wandering around the garden of your cottage. How did you get to the stones?"

"I was looking at the flowers while I had my cup of tea and I saw you go out. And then you disappeared and I thought you'd collapsed." Megan closed her eyes, remembering the feeling that had overtaken her. "I ran over to help you and when I got to the big stone monument thing something happened. I can't remember if I touched it but the most peculiar feeling came over me."

"What happened then?"

"I don't know." She stared through the gap in the trees to the next field. In the distance, the three grey markers were highlighted against the clear horizon.

A shiver ran through Megan and she leaned into David as he stopped and put his arm around her.

"Don't be frightened."

"If you tell me more about what's happening—or going to happen I might not be so bloody scared."

David looked up at the sun. "It's not quite midday. We've got some time."

"Time before what? You're talking in riddles." Megan's temper rose and she pulled away from him, ignoring the cold that trickled through her veins when she let him go. "All I know is I'm—we're—in 1971 and you're about to whisk me back to 2011. What's going to happen? Is some sort of time machine going to arrive and send me back home? Tell me, David." Fear cracked her voice and she shivered as the anxiety about the unknown snaked down her back.

David took her hand and led her over to the stone wall He turned, lifted her easily, and sat her on the flat stone on the top before sliding his guitar from his shoulder and placing it safely in the shade. Gently, he parted Megan's legs and stood between her thighs. The warmth of the stone beneath her legs was nothing compared to the heat that filled her when David leaned into her and held her waist gently.

"Last year—1970—I was touring the pub circuit in England. My songs were becoming well known and I'd played the pubs for a couple of years. I had made enough money to live comfortably in a flat in London." He held her gaze steadily. "I came down to Glastonbury to the festival and stayed at the pub, and that's when I met Bear and Slim." He held her gaze and Megan tried to focus on his words. His closeness was sending delicious quivers all over her. "We hooked up and played a set at the first festival. It was very informal back then. We put down an album after last year's festival and it sold really well. We got a publicist allocated to us by the record company. That's when everything started to come unravelled. Emma was an addict, and we got linked to drug rumours because of her actions."

Word for word, David—Davy—was reciting what she'd read in the article on the way over. As he spoke, his voice deepened and the hint of that sexy Welsh accent tinged his words. Her stomach fluttered and the ever-present heat pooled between her thighs as she stared back at him.

"Ken, the publican, told me about Rose Cottage being vacant and I moved in after we finished the tour after the album was released." He dropped his forehead to the top of her head. "Are you with me?" He lifted his head and looked at her. Their eyes were level and Megan nodded.

"I'm with you. It's 1971 and you played at the first festival, which if I'm working things out correctly was last year.

"So Bear and Slim live in the seventies and you live in the present. I mean, in 2011? This is doing my head in." Megan scrunched her nose trying to follow his explanation. "But they were at the pub here? I met them when I was having lunch? The other day when I arrived. That wasn't 1971. And I still don't know how you found the present." She shook her head at the confused thoughts. "I mean, how you found my time. Where I was yesterday."

I can't say what I mean.

"Do you know what I am trying to ask?" Relief flooded through Megan when David nodded.

"Yes, I do. Bear and Slim come to visit sometimes. The time gates let you cross both ways. And that's what we're about to do. We're in 1971 and we need to get back to 2011."

"But what about age? Look at me. I'm still twenty-five, or I think I am. How can I go forward and still be my age? I'm not even born yet." Megan shook her head and clutched David's arm. Panic strained her voice. "And Bear and Slim? They looked exactly the same when I met them the other day as they did in 1971. And you should be—what—how old?"

David put his hand on hers. "Age stays the same through the gates. I've done a lot of reading on it since Alice took me through the first time."

"Alice? Beth's Aunt Alice?"

"Yes, Alice showed me the gate when I lived next door to her. Her family has always known about it."

"Well, I don't think they know about it now. Beth hasn't ever been over here." Megan folded her arms across her chest. "So you're telling me that anyone who touches this stone can go back in time? And come back again? So why aren't there hundreds of people doing it? And why isn't it known about?"

David shook his head. "No. There seems to be some sort of mystical connection needed with others who have gone through. The only others I know who have crossed are Bear and Slim…and Alice who owns your cottage."

"So where is she?" Megan put her hand up to her face. "Is she here? Or there? Shit, I don't even know where here or there or then *is* anymore. It's just too much to take in." Thoughts were whirling through her head. "So what's the connection?"

"Bear and Slim and I are connected with our music. We started playing right before the 1970 festival. The first time I crossed I only stayed in 2008 for a few weeks. It almost did my head in. I know exactly how you're feeling now. But trust me, once you accept it, it gets easier."

"I know my music history. The Davy Morgan Band was formed in 1970 and played for the first time to a small crowd in Glastonbury the same week." Excitement trilled through her as she realised what had happened. "Do you mean to tell me I actually witnessed the Davy Morgan Band at their first *big* performance after the first album? The first non-pub performance? The actual Davy Morgan Band?"

"We actually did play a small set at the 1970 festival. It was more like busking. But 1971 is our big festival when we take off…or when we took off." He grinned. "And yes, you did see our first big performance, apart from the pub tour. And we were bloody good, if I say so myself."

Excitement rippled through Megan and she swallowed and put her hand up to her throat as she sought to understand. "I can't understand it. You—Davy Morgan—live in my time in the Cayman Islands. There are never any current photos of you. I've kept an eye out for years. I had a massive crush on you in my teens."

"That must be the connection between us. You knew me and my music." He stared at her and her lips parted as she waited for him to continue. "That's probably how the time gate opened for you." David held her gaze. "As much as I resisted it, I was drawn to you the instant I tripped over you on my porch. I guess that completed the connection between us that let you go through." He shrugged. "It's all an unknown. I just need to keep you safe."

"What was the connection between you and Alice?" She stared at him and he was the first to look away, and she wondered if they had been in a relationship. She waited for him to run his hand though his hair. She'd already figured out he did that when he was stressed. But he was looking past her, past the stone, and she couldn't see the expression on his face until he turned back to her.

"Alice supported me through a very hard time after our first record." Megan frowned at him and he held her gaze. "Last year, 1970. I took the blame for something. And she was a true friend when I needed one." David glanced up at the sky and the shadow moving across the front of the marker stone. "Come on. It's almost time to go."

Megan shivered and rubbed her arms as a cloud crossed the sun. "So how do we know where we are going to end up in the next few minutes?" She looked up at David.

Can I trust him? Her heart said she could, but her logical brain was screaming, *No.*

David put his arms around her and held her close. "All we have to worry about now is getting back safely." He lifted his head and squinted at the cloud obscuring the sun. "We have to make sure there is as little shadow as possible when we touch the stone. The less shadow and the closer to midday we can get, the smoother the transition. It's about two minutes away."

"Are you sure we can get back?"

David nodded. "Yes, I've done it many times now. Alice sent me alone, and Bear and Slim know the way themselves. I just haven't done it with anyone else so I'm not sure whether we'll go together or one at a time."

"And you're sure we will go back to where we came from?" Megan swallowed at the thought of ending up in some unknown time and place. It was bad enough here with no shoes and no money, but at least she'd found David and he knew what was going on. No wonder he'd been so frantic to find her.

"Yes, I'm sure." He pulled back, grasped her waist, and lifted her down to the grass. "Come on, it's time to go."

He touched her cheek gently. "Don't worry. I'll take care of you."

Chapter Eighteen

Kathy threw the phone on the bed and crossed to the window. She put her hand to her stomach and took a deep breath, trying not to stress. It wasn't good for the baby.

"Still no answer?"

She shook her head as Tony came over and put his arms around her. It was a bleak winter afternoon and rain droplets were running down the window panes. It made her feel like crying.

"It's okay, Kath. Megan will be fine. We know she got there safely."

"I've just got this feeling that something's wrong."

Tony stepped back and sat on the side of the bed. "There is. I'm getting nowhere with this appeal. I'm coming up with a dead end everywhere I look."

"What are you thinking?"

"Either Megan's guilty or we're dealing with someone who's covered all bases. The university have judged her on the evidence there is, and I won't lie to you. It's bad."

"But you know yourself that we paid for her ticket to London. You can prove that one."

He shook his head slowly. "Would you believe it's not on my Visa statement?"

"What?" Disbelief ran through Kath. "It has to be. You booked it online, didn't you?"

Tony ran his hand through his hair. "I did. But trust me it's not there. I've called the bank and they're looking into it."

A shiver ran down Kathy's back. "Tony. If someone goes to those lengths to make Megan look bad, he wouldn't try and hurt her, would he?"

Tony shrugged. "I wasn't going to say it. I didn't want to worry you, but the same thought crossed my mind. Thank goodness, she's overseas."

"I think it's time I went to the police. It's time they started looking into the activities of Greg Cannon. Christ, if he can log into the bank records what else is he capable of?"

"And *why* is he doing it?"

Fear filled Kathy as Tony shook his head. "I don't know. I don't think it's got anything to do with getting that job at the university. I am starting to think the guy's a nutter. I think he's done it because he can."

"You be careful, darling." Kathy put her arms around her husband.

"I'm going to go to the university now, and then I'm going to the police station. You keep trying to call Megan."

"I will. Just be careful."

Chapter Nineteen

A thrill of anticipation shot through Megan as they crossed the last field to the three large stones. Brooding and dark despite the midday sun, the ancient structures were silhouetted against the bright sky. For the first time, she noticed the row of small stones that completed the line. If David hadn't been holding her hand tightly, she knew it would have been fear consuming her rather than anticipation.

Would this strange connection between them last when they crossed back to her time? Or was it only because they were in the seventies? She hoped it wouldn't disappear. They had some unfinished business and the thought of that sent an exquisite pulse of heat shooting through her.

David stopped in front of her and pointed to the stones. "I've experimented over the last couple of years. Each of the stones works in exactly the same way."

"But what if you go the wrong way in time...in the wrong direction? You could end up anywhere."

"I know, I've thought of that. But there's only me. I live alone in the Caymans and no one depends on me for anything. I suppose I would look at it as an unexpected adventure."

"I know the feeling," Megan murmured.

"In fact, when we went to Taunton the other day, I was thinking how good it would be to go back to Norman times," he said. "But Alice warned me not to experiment."

"Don't confuse me. Just take me back home." Megan took a single step towards the stone but David pulled her back.

"No wait. We'll go together."

Securing his guitar firmly on his shoulder, David led her to the middle stone. They were close enough that the warmth of the stone heated her skin and an almost imperceptible humming filled the air. He turned and took her face between his hands.

"Don't touch the stone or lean against it until I say so. Okay?"

Megan nodded as she looked up into his dark eyes and his breath warmed her lips.

She stretched up on her toes and lightly brushed her lips against his.

"One kiss…just in case."

With a soft groan, David pulled her closer and his mouth ground against hers. She opened her lips and welcomed him as his heat filled her. Anticipation quivered through her as his tongue tangled with hers and she pushed against him, her breasts aching with the need to feel his bare skin against her. Reaching around, she ran her hands beneath his shirt and ran her fingers along his sun-warmed skin.

"Fucking hell." His words were hot against her lips. "How do you do this to me, Megan? You're a witch."

The need in his voice sent heat rushing through her, and she pushed closer to him. "I don't know," she said and her voice trembled. "I just know I need to touch you." The warm scent of his skin and the tight grip of his hands on her waist sent her head spinning. She knew he wanted her…or needed her…as much as she needed him. It was a physical craving and she'd never experienced anything like it before. She needed to be satisfied now.

"Quickly, let's go back," she said, need lacing her words.

David pulled away and stared at her intently for a long minute before he dropped his hands from her waist. She stepped back and the urgency of her sexual need faded a little as the physical connection between them was broken.

His voice was ragged and he gulped deeply as he turned to the middle stone.

"Go around to the back side in the shadow and put your hand against the stone. I'll follow you."

When Megan woke it was dark. Disoriented, she looked around the unfamiliar room. Fear crawled through her stomach as her eyes adjusted to the darkness. It was silent except for the loud ticking of an old-fashioned clock on the table in the corner of the room.

She was alone in a large bed, and it wasn't the bed in her room at Violet Cottage.

"David?" she called softly.

But all was quiet. Swinging her legs over the side of the bed, she grasped the edge as her head swam. Her eyelids began to droop and she forced them open.

She had to find out where she was. Or more importantly, *when* she was.

Pulling herself to her feet by holding on to the cold metal headboard, she fought the waves of weakness that washed over her. For a moment, her stomach roiled and she swallowed as saliva filled her mouth and she thought she would vomit. She closed her eyes and took a deep breath, and the feeling slowly receded. Letting go of the bed, she stood, opened her eyes, and the room blurred in front of her.

Forcing herself to move towards the door, she took short steps as the room swayed around her.

Where the hell am I and where is David?

The doorknob was icy beneath her hand. She turned it and let out a sigh of relief as the door opened. She peered around into a narrow corridor with a set of wooden steps at the far end. Faint light shone in from a small lace-covered window high in the wall above the steps. Her head steadied and she let go of the doorknob and walked slowly towards the stairs. A brighter light shone up from the room below.

"David?"

There was no answer and a sliver of fear trembled down her back. She definitely wasn't in her own cottage—or rather Alice's cottage. She could see that much in the dark. Walking quietly down the narrow staircase, she listened for any sound coming from below.

But all was quiet.

As she stepped onto the bottom step, the old timber groaned and a tall figure appeared from behind a sofa.

"Hell, Megan. You scared me. I thought you were still asleep." David's voice came across the room. She put her hand on her chest as her heart thudded hard and she took the final few steps to the old sofa in the middle of the room. David sat up against the cushions and the faint light shining in from the window reflected off his bare chest.

"What time is it?" Megan stood beside him and put her hand up to her head.

"Are you okay?" David stood and pulled her to him and the warmth of his skin rubbed against her bare arms. The horrid nausea and dizziness had taken all of her energy and she hadn't even looked to see what she was wearing when she'd woken upstairs alone. She was still in the same clothes she'd had on since she'd left the cottage.

However long ago that had been.

"Just a bit shaky. Like I felt when I woke up in the first aid tent…whenever that was. But not as bad." Megan leaned into him, and the shaking that had taken hold of her limbs slowed down and her heart slowly resumed its normal beat. "Where are we? Did it work?"

"We're at my cottage. You went out like a light when we came through the time slip." Although she stood in the circle of his arms, David's face was in the shadow and she couldn't see the expression on his face.

"I carried you back here and put you to bed so I could make sure you were okay. It's been a long night and I didn't want to wake you, so I slept down here."

"The night? How long have I been out?"

David dropped his arms and turned to the window. "Hear the blackbirds? Sun's about to come up."

"I lost half a day and a whole night?" Megan lifted her head and for the first time since she'd woken, the room didn't spin. Although her energy was coming back slowly, she was disoriented. It was like waking from a bad dream.

"Or did I? I feel so crazy asking this but...*when* are we?"

"Back where you started." David dropped his arms and Megan walked across to the window. The sky was a soft apricot and she could see the yellow roses tumbling over the fence between the two cottages. Mist hung low over the fields and the spire on Glastonbury Tor rose above the fingers of mist drifting beneath the hill. "You're back where you belong. I'll put some coffee on, or would you rather go back to your cottage for a shower?" David's voice was polite and Megan sensed he was trying to put some distance between them. The frantic need that had consumed her at the stones had gone and heat rose in her cheeks as she remembered the urgency of her demand that he take her back quickly. The sooner she got out of here the better. She needed to get her head together and figure out what had really happened to her.

"I'll just go back to my cottage, thanks. I'll have a coffee over there."

David gripped her arms and shook his head. "I want you to come back here. We need to have a talk about what happened and set some rules."

"Rules? What sort of rules?" She had no idea what he was talking about.

"You can't tell anyone what happened to you."

Megan laughed but there was no humour in it. "You think I'm going to go around telling the world I'm a time traveller? Give me credit for some sense. I'd be locked away."

Bitterness filled her as the events of the last couple of days came rushing back to her. "There's no need for me to talk about it. Your secret is safe with me. I've got enough problems already without adding to them."

So, all he was worried about was his secret getting out. No mention of the closeness they'd shared. She'd foolishly thought there'd been something special between them. Before they'd come through the time gate, she'd felt so connected to him.

Sucked in again. I do it every time.

A shaft of sunlight speared through the window and she turned to the door without looking at David. She didn't want to see the coldness that she knew would be in his expression. He'd gotten what he wanted from her, now that he'd gotten her safely back to the cottage. So now she would leave him to his own world. There was no need for him to make rules. No way was she going anywhere near that field again.

She still couldn't quite get her head around the whole David Morgan/Davy Morgan and the band thing, even though he'd explained it to her. There were so many questions she wanted to ask, but if he was going to withdraw from her and treat her as he had that first night, she'd find out another way. She'd go back to her laptop and look at all the files she had. There were tons of articles from the music magazines of the seventies.

"Suit yourself." His voice was clipped and he didn't smile. He walked over to the side of the room and picked up a T-shirt. "I'll walk you over just in case you're still a bit shaky on your feet."

Opening the front door, he stood back to let her through.

"Whatever."

By the time they reached Violet Cottage, the sun had cleared the eastern horizon and the morning had brightened. Megan ignored the arm that David held out to her and she strode around the side of the cottage. Her composure had come back quickly and she didn't need to hang on to him as she did before. She crossed to the garden and picked up the cup she had been drinking from the other day. It was still lying where she had dropped it when he'd disappeared.

"Thank you. I'm fine now." She opened the door, went inside, and tried to close it, but his boot blocked it.

"I'll give you a half hour and then I'll come over to check you're okay. I have to go back to the festival…we have a set to play later this morning," he said.

"There's no need, David." Megan kept her voice cold. Conflicting emotions ran through her and she needed some time to sort her head out. "I'm fine. Go and do whatever you have to do."

"I'll be back."

She shrugged and he removed his foot and walked away.

Megan leaned her head against the door for a moment. A hollow feeling gnawed at her stomach and she didn't think it had anything to do with hunger.

Of the food variety, that was.

Despite how the urgency of the sexual attraction had faded, strong feelings rioted through her. Her response to David was all mixed up with the love for the "rock star" icon she'd had as a teen, and her love of his music. Not only had she experienced that music live, she'd had hot sex with the idol from her teens.

Either that or she was crazy.

Shaking her head with disbelief, she walked upstairs to run a much-needed bath. Everything was the same in the pretty little bedroom. Her suitcase overflowed on the floor just as it had been.

When the bath was half-full, she turned the taps off and tipped in some bath salts that were on the windowsill above the old-fashioned pink bathtub. Slipping off her jeans and T-shirt, she stepped into the bubbles. Sliding down into the warm water was bliss and she rested her head on the back of the bath, closing her eyes as the water covered her.

Images of the last day flashed through her mind and she shook her head slowly from side to side. She reached for her loose hair and looped it in a top knot as it fell to her damp shoulders. She had time travelled back to the seventies and had watched Davy Morgan sing. She'd also had the best sex of her life with him on a riverbank at the festival.

As she thought about it, her nipples pebbled and the muscles between her thighs tightened. She'd been able to ignore it because she'd felt ill when she'd woken up next door, but now the sexual desire was back with a vengeance. Stepping from the bathtub, she towelled herself dry and shook her hair free. As she walked past the tiny hand basin, her reflection peered hazily back at her through the steam on the small round mirror. Her cheeks were flushed and her eyes were bright, her lips red and full. Excitement glimmered from the depths of her eyes and it mirrored the anticipation running through her body. She looked more alive than she had for the past year.

Her suitcase was on the floor and as she reached for it, a wave of dizziness overcame her. Dropping to the bed, she put her head between her knees and waited for the feeling to pass. At least she didn't feel sick this time. Her eyelids were heavy and she decided to close her eyes for just a moment before she got dressed.

Chapter Twenty

David knocked on the door and waited. He'd spent the past hour trying to decide how to handle this damned fire Megan had lit in him. He'd been deliberately distant when they'd come back through the time slip because he didn't want her to know how worried he'd been about her when she'd passed out. He'd sat next to her and watched her sleep once he'd put her in his bed, and it had taken all his willpower not to climb in beside her.

The past three days since she'd arrived in his life had turned his world upside down. His life had been settled and he'd been content with the way things were. He'd gotten over being blamed for Emma's death, and until Holly had shown him that bloody article, he'd managed to put it behind him. He enjoyed living in isolation in the Cayman Islands and coming over to his cottage every summer to go to a festival, do some touring, and put down a new album in the studio. Living and writing his music in the twenty-first century and slipping back to be a part of the seventies scene gave him the best of both worlds. Most importantly, he had the privacy to live his life exactly how he wanted and the royalties from the songs he was singing were keeping him very comfortable.

Until today, Bear and Slim, Clive, and of course Alice, were the only others who knew how he lived across the span of time. His two band members made a habit of coming back with him occasionally for a visit to the pub. The connection among them enriched their music.

And now dear Alice was gone.

Megan's knowing about the time slip could make things difficult. Putting herself in danger had brought the bad publicity surrounding Emma's death back with a vengeance. He needed to keep Holly in control, too. It was time to get another publicist if she was going to go for the sensational. All he hoped was that Holly hadn't seen Megan on the stage, because if she had, he was sure she'd plan some out there publicity about Davy's new woman. He snorted in disgust. This festival couldn't come to a close soon enough for him. The high from the music had been the usual buzz, but the double complication of the bad publicity and Megan's staying next door was doing his head in.

This connection to her and the urge to be with her was purely sexual. She'd gotten beneath his skin.

And into my head. And he didn't want to admit that she was on the way to his heart.

Once he checked she was okay, he was going to say goodbye. He knocked again and looked at his watch. There were only a couple more hours before he had to go back and join the guys for the next set. He would move on and put her behind him, too

"Megan? Are you there?" He lifted his hand and rapped his knuckles on the solid wooden door. When she didn't answer a frisson of fear rippled through him. He'd not seen anyone be so badly affected by going through the gates.

God, what if she'd passed out in the bath?

This time, he pounded on the door and when she didn't answer, he turned the knob. The door opened and he stepped in.

"Megan?"

Taking the stairs two at a time, David hurried along the narrow hall upstairs and looked through the open bathroom door. The bath was full of water and her clothes were on the floor but there was no sign of her. The panic subsided a little. Swivelling around, he headed for the bedroom and stopped in the doorway.

Megan was curled on her side in the middle of the bed wrapped in a pink towel. His heart kicked up a notch. One hand rested beneath her cheek and a rosy flush stained her skin. Crouching next to the bed, he ignored the blood pumping through him and placed his hand gently on her forehead and brushed the loose hair back from her face.

"Megan," he said softly. "Are you okay?"

She rolled over onto her back and stretched. "I'm fine. I fell asleep after my bath, but I feel great now." Looking up, she smiled and held his gaze. It was like getting a jolt of electricity through his entire body.

For the love of God, he couldn't keep away from her. With a groan, he buried his face in her hair and tried to contain the raging need that was coursing through his body. He'd thought he had it under control, but one look at her lying on the bed wrapped in a towel and all his good intentions flew out the window.

Standing up, he peeled his T-shirt off and threw it on the bed before stepping out of his jeans. He looked down at Megan—the intensity of her gaze had not left him and it held the same fire that was coursing through his body.

At the window, delicate lace curtains blew softly in the light morning breeze and the smell of roses filled the room as Megan reached a hand up to him. She kept her gaze locked on him without speaking.

Need rushed through him, and he closed his eyes. A thrum of need throbbed through his blood and this time he wanted to go slowly.

But damn it to hell, he had to be back with the band in an hour or so.

"Shit." He dropped down beside her onto the bed and stared at her. Her gaze raked him up and down as he hesitated.

"What's wrong?" Her voice was a low, throaty purr.

"I want to stay here with you, but I've only got a short time before I have to go. I don't want to rush you again." He ran his finger lightly up her stomach and covered the hand on her breast with his.

"Do you have to leave?"

David held his breath as Megan lifted her butt from the bed and pulled the towel away from around her. His gaze travelled down her body, past her full breasts and down past her flat stomach. In their swift coupling in the dark the other night, he'd not been able to see and appreciate her beauty.

"Yes." He dropped his mouth to her neck and nipped the delicate pale skin, and she gasped. "If I don't go back this time, it *will* change the future. Or what is my present. This is the set where we get

234

picked up by the agent and the band will take off. If I don't go—"

"Well, then, you'd better hurry up here and get on over there."

"Shit, why now of all times?" He took her mouth with his and slipped his tongue into the welcoming warmth. Time almost stood still and the need to leave went away…almost.

She reached her hands around his back and her nails scratched down his back.

***

Fifteen minutes later, David pulled his jeans on before leaning down to the bed and brushing Megan's lips with his. She pushed him away reluctantly— knowing he had to go. He stretched the black T-shirt over his head as he headed for the door and she smiled as he tripped over his boots and cursed. Picking them up, he stood in the doorway and smiled back at her.

"I'll be back about midnight. As soon as we finish. Wait up for me?"

"I've slept enough to stay awake for two days." Megan stretched as a delicious warmth coursed through her. "I'll go into the village, get some supplies, and make you dinner."

David frowned. "Don't go anywhere near the stones. Promise? I don't want to lose you again."

"Oh, there's no fear of that, don't you worry. I'll stick to the road and come straight back." She swung her legs over the side of the bed and wrapped the sheet around her. "Now go."

With one last reluctant look at her, David disappeared along the hallway, and when she heard the front door close, Megan went across to the window and grasped the sheet to her breast waiting for him to appear. After a couple of minutes, he came out of his cottage, dressed completely in black, with his guitar slung over his shoulder, and crossed the back garden. This time when he approached the stone markers and disappeared, she relaxed, knowing he was okay and where he had gone.

Wide awake and her energy renewed, she slipped into the bathroom for a quick shower before wandering downstairs. Even though she hadn't spent much time there, the cottage was beginning to feel like home. Thoughts of her real life and home seemed distant and the time she had spent with David filled her thoughts. She knew she'd surprised him with her sexual response this morning.

Hell, I surprised myself.

The effect he had on her physically and the way he made her feel were unlike anything she'd ever experienced before. The intensity of her feelings for him consumed her completely—body, heart, and soul.

As she headed for the kitchen, a muffled ringing reached her and it took a moment to realise it was her cell phone in her bag back in the living room. As she rummaged for it, a strange feeling came over her. It was as though it was someone else's bag. It was all familiar to her, but she felt distanced from everything, as though the time spent in the past had put a glass wall between the past and her present.

Shaking her head in an attempt to dispel the strange sensation, she pressed the phone to her ear.

"Hello?"

"Megan, where the hell have you been?" Kathy's voice came over the connection and she sounded upset. "I've been trying to call you for twenty-four hours and your phone just rang and rang every time."

"Sorry, I didn't take my phone with me to the…er…festival." Megan wandered over to the window, looking at the tents in the far distance as she tried to concentrate. "And it was dead for a couple of days too before I got an adapter, and the signal is really bad. A lot of stuff doesn't work right here."

"Tony wants to talk to you. It's not good."

"Okay. Put him on."

"Hello, Megan, I'm afraid the news isn't good. You're going to have to come home."

"I can't." It was the last thing Megan wanted to do at the moment.

"You have to." The irritation was evident in Tony's voice. "I've worked my butt off for you, and the disciplinary committee has agreed to hear your appeal in person. They've had a look at some of the evidence I've gathered from your files—mind you, there was very little to support your case—so you're lucky they're prepared to interview you. I think it's because the police are involved."

"The police?" Megan screwed her nose up as she walked across to the kitchen. The empty bottle from the red wine—was it only such a short time ago—was still sitting on the kitchen sink.

"Yes, I called in to see them the other day. One thing in your favour. Greg Cannon has a record."

"I can't come home yet." Megan tried to focus on Tony's words. It all seemed so long ago and far away. She couldn't summon any interest in what he was saying.

"What do you mean you can't come? I've done as much as I can without you. Jeez, Megan, what the hell is the matter with you? There's no point continuing your research if you don't come home. You won't have a job or a doctoral position at the university."

Megan didn't reply and for a moment there was silence at the other end of the phone and then Kathy came on again. "Megs, what's wrong? Why is Tony storming around slamming doors and glaring at me?"

"I told him I can't come home yet. The appeal hearing will have to wait."

"I'm sure Tony can work something out." She could hear Kathy's muffled voice speaking to Tony and it sounded as though she had her hand over the phone.

"How soon can you come home?" Kathy came back on.

"I don't know. I have some things to work out."

"Your research?"

"No, just some stuff." Megan began to get irritated. "Look Kathy, tell Tony I really appreciate what he's done, but I've got some other stuff to deal with that's far more important to me than my job."

Her sister's voice rose. "You've only been gone a few days and like Tony said your research will mean nothing if you don't have a job. It's your whole career, Megan. If you want to save your skin, you'll have to come home to the meeting. What's happened over there that's more important?"

It was as though Kathy was now the mouthpiece for Tony, and Megan decided it would just be easier to agree.

"Yes, okay, whatever Tony thinks. I'll come home then. I'll let you know when I'm coming. And now I have to go. Good-bye."

Megan terminated the call before her sister could object, and she turned the phone off before throwing it back in her bag. It surprised her that there was any battery life left on the phone, anyway.

But then she thought about it. It had only been a couple of days since she'd charged it.

So much had happened to her in the last forty-eight hours.

Her whole life had changed, and she had a lot of things to work out before she flew back home for any hearing. She wasn't sure what she wanted yet, but before she made any decisions, she had a festival to go to.

And a man to consider.

Time would tell. That's what she needed…time to get her head around everything.

Chapter Twenty-One

"Fuck, man. We thought you weren't coming." Bear was behind the drums at the back of the stage and he watched David as he hurried to the amplifiers and plugged in his guitar, with only seconds to spare.

He turned and grinned at the drummer. "I wouldn't have missed tonight. I know how important this concert is. Tonight's our big night." Pulling the guitar strap over his shoulder, he nodded to the announcer, who'd been waiting at the microphone to announce the band.

Energy flowed through David's body and his nerves were jumping. As hard as it had been to leave Megan and come back through the time slip, his fingers were itching to play tonight. The music was flowing through him and he knew this was going to be the performance of his life. He could thank Megan for that.

Maybe it was all part of a bigger plan. Meeting Megan, getting inspiration for his performance, meeting the agent after the concert. Even without being forearmed with the knowledge of the performance tonight, he would have known that they were going to pull off a top-class performance.

It was a shame Megan couldn't be here to watch them, but the journey through the stones seemed to take so much out of her. He wasn't going to risk her travelling again.

Ever.

As soon as he was finished here, he was going straight back to her.

David launched into the first riff, the mellow music introducing the first words of his signature song, and the crowd cheered as they recognised the tune. A familiar face caught his attention and he frowned. Alice stood at the end of the front row in the middle of a group of young girls. She was dressed in a bright-red dress and her hair was braided beneath her red hat. Smiling up at him, she swayed with the music and David shook his head. He hadn't expected to see her here tonight.

Three songs later, the perspiration was dripping from him and when he pulled his shirt off, the crowd went wild. The number of people watching them had grown as they'd played and the word must have spread across the festival site. Music lovers had left the other stages and had come to listen to the Davy Morgan Band. He caught Slim's eye and the bass guitarist grinned at him and gave him a thumbs-up.

Looking down at the crowd as he sang, David detached himself from the words and just let it flow. He wondered which one of the onlookers was Mick Rothman, the agent who would come and see them after the concert and get them an amazing record deal. Knowing what was going to happen before it did was bizarre, but he'd read about the deal that happened tonight in his biography and now that he had come through the time slip, he was creating the present.

There was no way he was going to jeopardise what was about to happen. His future depended on it.

Past, present, and future all ran together as David put everything he had into the last song. The final chord crashed down and when he dropped his guitar and bowed to the crowd, they screamed and whistled. A flurry of movement at the front caught his attention. Two first aid workers leaned over someone lying on the ground and as the crowd stepped back to give them room, he saw Alice's bright-red dress spread out on the ground around her as the men worked on her.

"Shit."

As he turned and ran for the stairs at the back of the pyramid stage, a small man in a suit with a thin black moustache held his hand out to David.

"Davy Morgan? I'm Mick Rothman and I'd like to talk to you."

"Bear? Slim?" He called to the two band members who were unplugging their equipment before the next band came onto the stage. "Come and talk to Mr Rothman here. I'll be back up as soon as I can."

The agent frowned as David ignored his outstretched hand and he ran down the stairs as quickly as he could. Pushing through the crowd, he ignored the girls whose hands slipped off his sweaty, bare chest as they grabbed at him. When he reached the first aid men on the ground next to Alice, he dropped to his knees next to her.

"Alice? What's wrong?" She lay on her back with her eyes closed. Her face was pale and covered with a sheen of perspiration, and her hands were grasped tightly in front of her chest.

"We've called for the ambulance. We think she's taken something and had a reaction. Blood pressure is through the roof. Do you know who she is?" The younger of the two men looked at him and his eyes widened as he recognised David.

Before he could answer, Alice's eyes fluttered open. "Davy? Is that you? Don't leave me. Come with me?" Her voice was weak and she struggled to catch her breath. "Please? I'm scared. Don't let them take me away from here."

David reached out and took her hand between his. "Of course, I won't leave you. I'll look after you, don't worry, Alice."

The flashing red lights of the ambulance reflected on the side of the stage. David looked up and groaned. Not only was he going to be late getting back to Megan, but he was missing out on the meeting with the agent, Mick Rothman.

But he wouldn't leave Alice. There were too many things that could go wrong if he let her go to the hospital by herself.

Too many explanations that may be needed.

God, Alice, please don't die on me.

"I'll be back in a minute." He looked across at the paramedics who were placing an oxygen mask over Alice's mouth and nose. "Please wait for me."

Pushing through the milling crowd who were waiting for the next band to come on stage, he tore around the front of the stage and up the stairs, holding onto the flimsy hand rail as he took them two at a time. Mick Rothman frowned as he spoke to Bear and Slim. When David pushed past him and picked his T-shirt up from the floor, the agent smiled.

"Ah, at last." He stood back and waited for David to join the group.

"Sorry guys. They're taking Alice to hospital and I have to go in the ambulance. Whatever you think,

245

just take the deal and I'll agree with whatever you decide." He held Bear's gaze with his. "As long as you take the deal tonight. Okay?"

The burly drummer slapped him on the back as he headed back towards the stairs. "That's cool, Davy. Look after the old lady. Give her a kiss from me."

"Keep an eye on my guitar, please guys?" David pointed to his black Fender on the floor where he'd put it before he'd run to see if Alice was alright. Already it was getting lost amongst the equipment as the next band set up for their performance.

"Sure thing." Slim strolled over and picked it up as David headed back down the stairs.

Alice was already in the back of the ambulance covered with a white blanket. When David climbed in the back and sat beside her, she reached out and gripped his hand.

"Thank you, David. I'm a bit scared. They're taking me into Taunton hospital." Her eyes were wide and her hair had fallen from her braid over her face. "I've never been anywhere but Glastonbury. "Now I mean."

"I know what you mean." David squeezed her hand as he glanced across at the ambulance driver. "Neither have I. We'll do it together."

He spoke confidently to keep Alice calm, but inside his thoughts were churning. He had no idea what would happen if they ventured too far away from the time slip and coming up with an ID for Alice was going to problematic. If they looked up her records, they'd find that she should only be about thirty years old.

Chapter Twenty-Two

Megan summoned up the courage to walk along the road into the village in the mid-afternoon. She gave the fields a very wide berth and was relieved when the bell on the shop door chimed as she pushed it open. Crazy Jules greeted her with a smile and Megan let out the breath she'd been holding.

"So, how's your water, then, dear?"

"Fine, thank you." She grinned at the woman, who was wearing brightly patterned tights beneath a lime-green apron today. "Solstice fixed it just as you said it would."

Not to mention the sexy rock star who fixed my pump. But she'd go along with the woman's story.

Picking up a basket, Megan wandered around the dim store, collecting the ingredients for a meal to have ready for David late tonight. Tomatoes, dried herbs, some bacon, and a jar of cream, as well as a packet of pasta, all went into the small plastic crate. She'd venture into the little cellar and raid Alice's wine stash, too.

She daydreamed as she poked about the store.

A pretty tablecloth and some flowers from the garden.

"Do you have any candles?" She placed the basket on the counter and began to unload her purchases.

"To take to the festival?" Jules turned around to a shelf behind the counter and picked up a small torch. "Safety wardens won't let you light candles there. Here's a torch for you, luv."

"Thanks, but not for the festival. For a romantic dinner."

God, where did that come from? She was usually a private person and here she was blabbing out her intentions.

Like an adolescent who had a crush on a rock star.

A cold feeling began in the pit of her stomach and she stopped unloading the goods while one hand gripped the handle of the basket. How often had David picked up a fan and spent time with her after a performance? She'd read about performers who used sex to come down from the music high.

Did he just take advantage of me? It had been like one of her teenage dreams come to life.

"You alright, luv?" Jules was looking at her curiously and she lifted her eyes slowly to the older woman's face. Her gaze was kind and Megan nodded.

"Yes, thanks, I'm fine."

And I will be. She'd been a willing participant in the whole episode and she just had to take him on trust.

But maybe she'd give the candles a miss. He'd probably run a mile if he thought she was trying to be romantic.

##

Megan stepped back and looked at the table setting. In the end, all she'd done was put a couple of place mats down and placed a jar of yellow roses in the centre of the table. The aromatic sauce was bubbling on the stove and her stomach grumbled. Hunger was gnawing at her but she'd wait for David. It was almost midnight and he should be back soon. In a way, she regretted not going back with him to see the performance, but based on the last two trips through the time slip, she would probably have slept through the entire performance anyway.

A bottle of red wine sat decanting on the table and she walked over to the window above the sink. In the distance, blue light bathed the spire on Glastonbury Tor. There was so much to see here and she intended

250

to do as much sightseeing as she could before she went back home to Sydney.

Home.

It was hard to focus on her life *before* the past two days. There were only a couple of days left of the festival. She really should go to the festival she'd come to attend. Then she would focus on going home and sorting out her appeal.

Maybe David could come with me?

Shaking her head, she determined to do some work towards her thesis. Her research since she'd arrived was non-existent. She must get herself out of this thrall she seemed to be caught in. Guilt rippled through her as she thought about how she'd ended the call to Tony and Kathy. Her brother-in-law had only been trying to help her and she'd cut him off. In the morning, she'd call and apologise, and explain why she couldn't come home.

But how to explain what had happened to her?

I don't really care about my job and my life at home because I've fallen in love with the rock star of my teenage dreams? Not to mention the time travel that had gotten her into that situation.

God. They'd lock me up. Then she replayed the words she'd just admitted to herself.

Fallen in love. Where the hell did that *come from?*

A noise outside caught her attention and Megan's heart accelerated as she hurried over to the door with a smile. She opened the door and looked out into the dark, but there was no one there. The scuffling continued but it must have been a small animal in the garden.

Disappointment overcame the impatience filling her chest. She wished he'd hurry up. The anticipation was becoming unbearable. Lowering the flame on the old gas stove, she gave the sauce a stir and filled another pan with water ready to cook the pasta as soon as he came in.

After pouring a glass of wine, she went outside and sat on the back porch to wait. Even though it was midsummer, the night was cool and the stars glistened in the clear sky. In the distance, the soft music of the current festival drifted across the fields, broken only by the occasional low moo of a cow.

Sipping her wine, she waited...and waited...and waited.

##

By 3:00 a.m. and two glasses of wine, the table on the porch was wet where the dew had begun to settle. Anger had replaced Megan's disappointment. Picking up the glass, she pushed open the kitchen door and went inside. She turned the stove off and tipped the water out of the pasta pot, tapping the pot loudly on the old stone sink to vent some of her disappointment.

God. How gullible am I?

David had obviously found someone else to take care of his needs. What was the saying?

Any port in a storm?

Too restless to sleep, she turned on her laptop and pulled up her files, curious to read the old articles about the festival and David, now that she could see him from a different perspective. First, she pulled up the newspaper headline she had seen in the village store.

Her chest closed and tears welled in her eyes as she read about the death of the band's publicist in 1970. As much as she'd known about his past from her reading over the years, it was the first time that had been mentioned. That piece of information had been omitted from his biography.

Oh, no, the poor guy. No wonder he'd been so gruff when she'd first met him. She scrolled through the rest of the files that the librarian had scanned and e-mailed to her.

Her breath caught as she gasped. An article from 'It's Here and Now' had the sensational headline *Davy Loves the Ladies.* Below the headline was a photo of David and a woman in a tight clinch on the stage. Her head whirled and she closed her eyes.

It was her. Someone had taken a photo of them when David pulled her into his arms after the concert. A feeling of unreality tore at her and she struggled to catch her breath. It was only a photo of the back of her, but she knew it was her because she had been there.

David. Where are you?

Megan scrolled through the rest of the article, and the warmth disappeared as she read the words and the sad truth settled in her stomach like a stone.

Davy Morgan rushed to the hospital to be by the side of his new woman the very night after he was pictured in the arms of the mysterious auburn-haired beauty. He loves to love 'em and leave 'em, does our Davy.

Megan snapped the lid of the computer shut, drained her wine, and went to bed.

The next morning, she lay in bed as dawn broke. A languor had taken over her limbs and she stayed in bed as the light on the white walls of the small bedroom turned a rosy pink. Just as when she'd had sex with David on the riverbank. During the couple of hours sleep she'd snatched, her dreams had been full of him, and she was reluctant to leave her bed where she felt so close to him.

Singing to me, touching me…
Promising he'd come back.

She pulled herself out of her dream, reminding herself of what she'd read and how she'd been sucked in. Megan dragged herself out of bed, determined to forget David and go to the festival.

Well, he didn't come back. It's time to get on with my research, and get on with real life. Forget this dream existence and go to the festival.

The bloody 2011 festival.

She dressed in a pair of jeans and a T-shirt, put on a pair of sneakers, gathered her recorder and notebook, and set off up the road. When she walked past Rose Cottage, she couldn't help looking for him. She strolled past slowly and peered in. But the door was closed and there was no sign of life.

Surely he'd come back safely? A cold glimmer of fear trickled down her back, but she pushed it back. He'd been coming through the time slip for years. He knew what he was doing.

He's a big boy, Megan. He'll be okay.

And there are obviously plenty of other women to worry about him.

Today the village was jam-packed with vehicles and sightseers heading toward the old abbey. Modern vehicles, SUVs, and small cars. Obviously, the overflow from the festival had come to the village. Yesterday had been so much quieter but per the program, Megan knew today was the day when all the

255

big-name bands were playing. That explained all the cars and the crowds.

But despite that, she knew there'd be no David Morgan appearing.

Megan made her way through the crowds and along the road to the farm at Pilton. It was so different from when she'd wandered along here in her bare feet only yesterday…or actually it was different than what it looked like in 1971—more than forty years ago.

But now she needed to do what she had come here for and then book the first flight back to Australia. She needed to sort out her job.

Her thesis took priority and the wealth of information she had collected at the 1971 festival yesterday needed to be written down out of her head and into her notes before she forgot it.

Megan stayed at the festival for two hours before she headed back through the village, disillusioned. The 2011 festival didn't have the vibe of the one she'd been to yesterday. Slick and commercial, it was full of advertising billboards, parking attendants, and security men checking every bag that was carried through the gate. The crowds were quiet and boring, and the music was modern and did not touch her soul.

She refused to admit to herself it was because David wasn't there. It was simply different music, in a different time.

My expectations were way off base. But at least it was all material for her thesis.

Retrieving the key from the front porch, she put it in the door and glanced across at Rose Cottage wondering if David had come back.

It didn't matter. She was going home.

Chapter Twenty-Three

They kept Alice in the hospital in Taunton for two days while they ran tests and David almost went stir crazy. Luckily his wallet had been in his jeans pocket and he had enough money on him to get back to Glastonbury. Each day he spent with Alice at the hospital and he pumped her about her relatives in Australia.

He was worried Megan would think he'd let her down. He was sure Megan would be gone when he got back—if he got back. He'd promised her he'd be back that night, and he knew exactly what she'd think. The debauched rock star act he'd put on when he'd met her would help convince her he was unreliable and had just been using her.

Christ, what bad timing.

But there was no way he was letting her go.

"My niece, Joanna, lives in Sydney and I left the cottage to her." Alice was looking better this morning and her cheeks were back to their pink rosy hue. "She had a couple of small children before I stumbled on the time slip and lost touch, so I guess the friend your lady talked about must be my great niece."

"But do you know her surname? It wouldn't be McLaren would it?" David persisted. He was determined to get every scrap of information he could—just in case he needed it to find Megan.

"Yes, it is." Alice tugged on the old-fashioned strap hanging in front of her and pulled herself up higher on the pillow. "She's a bit of a radical like I was in my own time. She kept her own name after she married. I think her children took her name as well, because she divorced soon after she moved to Australia."

The door opened and the doctor came in carrying a clipboard. "Good news, Miss McLaren. You're right to go home. All your tests are clear and we can discharge you. It was only a bit of over-excitement that caused you to faint. You are in remarkably good health for a woman your age."

Alice winked at David and had her feet on the floor slipping on her shoes before the doctor had finished speaking. "Wonderful. Just get me my red dress out of the cupboard there, David, and we'll be on our way."

After she disappeared down the hallway to the bathroom, the doctor turned to David. "Do you have far to travel?"

David cleared his throat and looked away. "Ah. Yes, you could say that."

##

Getting Alice back to the village of Glastonbury was problematic and it was late afternoon before they stepped off the bus from Taunton. The bus stop was at the end of the lane leading to the cottages.

"Are you sure you'll be okay?" David hated the thought of leaving Alice and going back through the time slip and not knowing what would happen to her.

"You heard the doctor. Just a bit of overexcitement." She shoved him gently towards the door after he saw her into Violet Cottage. "Now you get back to your time and find that young lady of yours. Don't you go worrying about me."

"Can I use your phone before I go? I need to call the—"

"Sorry, dear. I don't have a telephone. You'll have to use the phone box in the village."

David reached out and took the elderly lady in his arms. "You take care, Alice." Her cheek was soft beneath his and she reached up and held his face between her hands.

"I was meant to meet you at the festival last year." She stared at him intently. "It all happens for a reason you, know. I am sure the only reason you met me was so you could find your young woman when the time came. Now you go and find your Megan."

With a last wave to Alice, David walked back along the road to the village and stopped at the red phone box outside the post office. He pulled Bear's phone number from his wallet and dialled, smiling as he tried to fit his fingers in the circular numbers to turn the old-fashioned dial mechanism.

The phone picked up on the first ring and Bear's sleepy voice came over the line. "Hello?"

"Bear, it's Davy."

"Hey, man. How's the old lady?"

"She's fine. Everything's good." David stared out over the village as the sun dropped towards the hills and golden clouds streaked the pink sky to the west. "How did you go with Rothman?"

"We celebrated most of the night." The guitarist's voice was excited. "You did it, man. Your singing clinched the deal. That performance was unreal. Mick's drawing up the contracts now and wants us in the studio in London as soon as the festival is over. We'll start recording our next album. Mick wants the first single released before the end of summer."

David let go of the breath he'd been holding. The first single of the Davy Morgan Band, which was their first big hit, had been released in the middle of July 1971.

It seemed everything was on track. As long as they recorded the single, it would all be okay. All he had to do was turn up to the studio. At least he knew he could get to Taunton in 1971. What he wasn't quite so sure about was if he could go back through the ley lines now. It was the longest he'd ever stayed away without going through the stones. His future and his income for the next forty years were secure. And then he could go back to 2011 and the island. But first, he needed to say goodbye to Megan and let her go.

"Okay, I'll make sure I'm back here by then."

After making arrangements to meet Bear at the Glastonbury pub next week, David placed the solid black receiver into the cradle and stepped out of the small red phone box.

Then he had to find Megan. David stepped outside and looked at the sky. Not long to go. Now he had to get to the stones and hope like hell Megan was still at the cottage. He had to cut ties with her for good—in both times.

Taking a shortcut through the back of the village, he followed the same path he had taken with her only yesterday. It seemed as if years had passed. The sun was bright and the cows looked at him curiously as they munched on the grass while he strode past, his guitar slung over his shoulder. The sun reached its zenith and he stepped to the back of the middle stone and placed his hand on the surface, still warm from the sun.

Chapter Twenty-Four

She was gone.

The cottage was empty.

Silence surrounded him.

David welcomed the despair that settled over him like a dark shroud.

It was for the best. Megan had her own life and her own future. He had his success and his life and his privacy with no worries about anyone in the Caymans. He leaned forward in the chair, dangling his hands between his knees. He had songs to write and music to record. His life would be full. So why did he feel so fucking empty?

It *was* for the best. He had to convince himself of that. Rubbing his hand through his hair, he stood, picked up his guitar, and opened the front door. He stared at Violet Cottage as the rays of the setting sun highlighted the yellow roses spilling over the fence between the two homes. If he closed his eyes he could still see her wandering through the garden.

He pushed open the gate to Alice's place and smiled as a whiff of sandalwood brushed by him. He'd just sit over here for a while and play some music.

As the sun dropped below the horizon and the sounds of night surrounded him, David closed his eyes and began to sing. He let the words come from his heart and the music soothed him.

The song flowed and he faced the truth as the night passed. He had to learn to open his heart. Now he'd found Megan. He'd fought falling for her, trying to use the time barrier as an excuse, but as he sat on Alice's patio, trying to be close to Megan, he admitted the truth.

I love her. And I need her in my life.

At midnight he put the guitar aside and stood, looking out over the dark garden. An owl hooted, breaking the silence, and he smiled.

Megan was responsible for herself, and she had known what she wanted. The connection between them was meant to be…and he had let her go.

"I know you're gone, Alice, but maybe you were right?" he whispered into the still night.

Maybe I can find happiness?

So all I have to do is bring her back to me.

It was time to write the words that would bring Megan back to him.

Chapter Twenty-Five

"Well done, Megan." Tony hugged her before they left the small office outside the vice-chancellor's suite. Miss Robinson, the vice-chancellor's secretary, pursed her lips in disapproval and Megan was tempted to blow a raspberry at the old cow. Instead, she smiled sweetly but got a rude grunt in reply.

The hearing had been rescheduled to allow her enough time to fly back from England, and she'd left the cottage as soon as the festival was over. Winning her case after only one meeting with the disciplinary committee was a huge victory, and she grasped the written letter of apology from the vice-chancellor between her fingers. Greg Cannon had been dismissed for making false allegations and hacking her password, and Megan had been totally cleared of any wrongdoing. The police record had been the key; Greg Cannon was a false name and he'd falsified the documents and qualifications to get the job at the university. His computer hacking skills had been tracked on an audit trail, and he'd been charged with numerous offences.

Megan's trip back to London on the train, and then the flight back to Australia were a blur. And now, not only had she got her job back with a good shot at the permanent promotion she also had the excitement of getting her notes out and working on her thesis with the wealth of material she'd picked up in Glastonbury.

Life *would* be good.

"Celebratory drink?" Tony glanced down at his watch. "Kathy and Beth should be at the pub by now. Kathy's looking forward to finally hearing all about your trip."

"I don't know, Tony." Megan smiled at him apologetically when he opened the glass door at the end of the corridor leading to the parking garage. "I think I'd prefer to go straight home. I'm really keen to get to work on my thesis."

"Come on, Megan, you've been home three weeks and you've been avoiding us like the plague. Kathy's been trying to get you over for dinner for the past two weekends. She's upset that you haven't even asked how the pregnancy is going."

The last thing Megan wanted to do was talk about the trip to Glastonbury. While she hugged the thought and the memory of Davy to herself, he stayed real to her. For some strange reason, she felt that if she talked about her experiences at Glastonbury, she would wake

267

up and realise it had all been a dream. For the time being, she didn't want to share it with anyone. On her living room wall, she'd put up a huge poster of Davy and had spent hours looking at it since she'd come home. His smouldering dark eyes followed her around her apartment.

Now that she'd won her appeal, and knowing she still had a job, maybe she'd get back to normal.

And forget him. It had been a pleasant visit and a once-in-a-lifetime experience that she couldn't tell anyone about…

Maybe spending time with her sister would help.

"Okay, just one drink."

The Oaks Hotel at Neutral Bay was crowded and Megan was greeted by a few friends as Tony led her out to the small bar at the back. Kathy was sitting with Beth at a table by an artificial log fire and she jumped up when Megan and Tony entered the room.

"Such great news!" Kathy hugged her. "You must be so relieved."

"Yes, It's a huge relief. I couldn't have proved it was Greg without Tony's help."

"What a bastard," Kathy said.

"Yes, and apparently, he's done it before. I was just unlucky enough to be in his sights."

"No one needs to worry for a while," Tony said as he lifted his glass. "The police said with his previous record, he'll go to prison this time."

"Now tell us all about the festival." Beth looked at her eagerly. "And I want to hear all about my Great-Aunt Alice's cottage. Was it quaint?"

Megan sat down and waited for Tony to bring her a glass of wine from the bar. She picked up the drink and the light caught the deep red of the wine in her glass. She closed her eyes, the memory of sharing the bottle of vintage red wine at the cottage with David filling her thoughts. A warm hand on her forearm alerted her to her sister's concern and Megan opened her eyes. Kathy was looking at her with a frown wrinkling her forehead.

"Megs, what's wrong?" Kathy leaned in and spoke softly to her while Tony and Beth chatted on the other side of the table. "You're pale and listless and not yourself. Winning the appeal should have put a bit of spark back in you. We've been worried about you since you came home." Kathy's face was full of concern. "I thought it was the case but it's not, is it? What's happened? You're not sick, are you?"

"I met someone in England." Megan's throat ached and her eyelids pricked with tears as she finally put David into words. The emotion she'd kept bottled

269

inside her tumbled through her and she put her hands against her chest. "Oh Kathy, I miss him so much."

"You were hardly over there long enough to meet anyone."

"Oh, believe me—it seemed like a very long time." Megan gave a short laugh. "Don't worry about me, Kath. I think I've picked up some sort of bug. I'll be fine."

For the rest of the night, she put everything she had into being sociable, asking Kathy about the nursery she was decorating, and the baby clothes she was knitting. By the time she got home, Megan was exhausted. She collapsed onto the lounge and flicked on the CD player with the remote and lay back as Davy's voice surrounded her. The words washed over her and she drifted off for a few moments until the mellow notes of the last song woke her.

How can I live without him?

Suddenly, she sat bolt upright and listened to the song.

Really listened.

She'd known this song since she was a teenager and hadn't taken much notice of the words but had smiled at the title. It had been the first Davy Morgan song she'd ever heard and it had caught her attention because it was called "For Megan."

Jumping up from the sofa, she went over and flicked through the old albums on the floor by the bookcase. Pulling out *Wandering,* his second album, she turned it over and read the back of the sleeve.

Excitement began to build in her stomach as she looked at the dates. "For Megan" had been written in early July 1971 and released as the last song on their big hit album. It said it was recorded at the studio in London and had been written by Davy Morgan alone.

The CD clicked back to the first song, but with shaking fingers Megan pressed the button on her stereo to select "For Megan." Sitting on the floor in front of the stereo so she could go back as soon as the song finished, she listened to it again and again. Grasping the album cover in her hands, her lips moved as she read the words of the song written on the back cover.

Certainty filled her and she relaxed, taking deep breaths. A lightness filled her chest and she smiled. The words of the song *had* been written for her. She was sure they had, as sure as the breaths she was taking in would sustain her. Something must have happened to keep David from coming back to her that night. There was no girlfriend—that was newspaper gossip. It wasn't because he'd been taking advantage of her. He'd had the same intense feelings she did.

Maybe she should have waited, or maybe he hadn't been able to get back at all. She had to trust.

Come back to me, Megan.

Together we will conquer time.

He'd written the song to get the message to her. The tension that had filled her body since that night slowly eased out of her body and her limbs relaxed as the chorus swelled.

Come back to me, I can't find you.

I need you, I love you.

The song ended and Megan clicked the stereo off. With surprise, she reached up to her wet cheeks. She'd been so immersed in the words of his song for her, that she hadn't even been aware she was crying. Wiping her eyes, she logged on to her laptop. There were flights to book and she would have to apply for more leave from the university. The only problem she could foresee was finding David if he hadn't been able to get back through the time slip. If it meant she had to go back in time again, so be it.

Whatever she had to do to find David, she would do it.

Chapter Twenty-Six

"McLaren." David tried to keep his tone patient as he spelled out the surname. He'd spent two days scouring the Internet for all the McLarens he could find in the Sydney white pages, and last night he had spent hours dialling Australian phone numbers. No one had heard of a Beth McLaren, and he was beginning to wonder if he'd remembered the name that Megan had said correctly.

Now he was onto the local borough and trying to get the Australian address of the owner of Violet Cottage, but had come head-to-head with British bureaucracy.

"Yes, sir, that is correct. The owner is Ms McLaren in Australia, however I cannot divulge her address. It is against the privacy law. I probably shouldn't even confirm that name for you."

"But what if I wanted to buy the cottage?" David was prepared to do anything to find out a way to get in touch with Megan.

"You would have to contact the solicitor who manages the cottage."

Thank God. Finally, he was making progress.

"So can you give me that name and number?"

"Certainly, sir. Just give me a moment." Over the phone line, keys clicked as the clerk retrieved the information and finally came back to give him the name of a law firm in London.

Two phone calls later and he had managed to get an assurance that an e-mail would be sent to Ms. McLaren asking her to contact him.

The morning after he'd written Megan's song, he'd gone down to the village and discovered that Jules' husband, Ned, the village taxi driver, had driven Megan to the train station to catch the train to London.

No privacy issues there. Jules knew all about Megan's plans as Ned had relayed them back to her. Megan had gone straight to Heathrow and would be back in Australia by now.

Christ Almighty. I don't even know her last name.

##

"One of your best, man." Bear nodded at David as his fingers strummed the last notes of "For Megan" and Mick Rothman gave them a broad smile through the glass wall of the studio. David had written the song for Megan in the cottage the day before he'd

274

come back through the stones to meet Bear and Slim, and they'd headed off to the studio. The trip had been cramped in Bear's van overflowing with their instruments and amplifiers.

One more song to record and the album was finished. Mick was ecstatic and he was predicting a hit album. David didn't tell him that three of the songs would reach number one in the States over the summer and challenge the Beatles for the longest place in the number one spot.

Knowing his future when he was back here was surreal. He came back occasionally to play the festivals and record some more albums—and they did a hugely successful tour, but mostly he stayed in the twenty-first century.

Bear wouldn't make it through the eighties, but he hadn't shared that with the guys either. He'd found his grave in the small village cemetery in Glastonbury when he'd read about the lives of the band on Wikipedia.

"We're done. Fabulous job, guys." Mick opened the door of the studio, the cigarette that was permanently in his mouth hanging from the corner. "Now, to the promotion. I've scheduled an appearance in London for you guys next week."

David shook his head. "Right, I'll make sure I'm back by then."

"Back from where?"

David caught Bear's and Slim's grins and he shrugged as he lifted his guitar from his shoulder. "I might sound arrogant, but we'll be big. Trust me." He walked over to Bear and held out his hand. "I've organised a lift back to Glastonbury."

Bear held his eye and David could tell he understood that they wouldn't see him for a while.

"Take care, man. It's been fun."

Slim walked over and punched him lightly on the shoulder. "You look after yourself, man. Have fun spending all that dosh."

David grinned at the look on Mick's face. His mouth was hanging open and the cigarette had dropped from his mouth.

"Bye, Mick."

***

The second time the taxi dropped her off in front of the cottages, Megan walked up the shady lane leading to Violet Cottage and she knew where she was going, and didn't end up on the wrong porch. Her stomach fluttered and her heart pounded as she walked past David's place. His front door was closed and all was quiet, but she wasn't going to let that bother her. It was a brilliant late-summer morning and the slight breeze ruffled the shiny green leaves on the hedge lining the narrow laneway.

David had written the song for her to get her back, and now she was here, and they would find each other somewhere, somehow, in some time. That was the one thing she was sure of. A tremble went through her as she thought of going back through the stones. She walked around to the back of the cottage and put her bag down on the porch, closing her eyes as the heady perfume of the roses surrounded her.

The faint mooing of the cows in the field at the back of the cottages drifted across on the breeze and she put her hand up to her eyes and peered back across towards the village. Glastonbury Tor stood tall in the morning sun, and the last drifts of mist around the three marker stones were gradually disappearing in the light breeze. The brightly coloured tents of the festival had long gone and an idyllic English countryside spread out before her. With a happy sigh, she turned to the door, but paused as a flash of movement near the monument caught her attention.

Her breath caught as a familiar figure in a black T-shirt and black jeans stepped from behind the middle stone. Even from this distance, the sunlight highlighted the blue-black lights of his long curls. She waited with her heart thudding in her chest as he crossed the field to the gate at the back of Rose Cottage. She pressed her lips together and rubbed her arms as a lightness filled her entire body.

Finally, Megan stepped from the porch onto the soft grass and waited for David to see her. He stopped and stood stock-still. He turned his head slowly towards her and the expression on his face was all she'd dreamed of. His dark eyes lit up and those sexy full lips tilted in a huge grin. A surge of warmth began in the pit of her stomach and rose to her chest.

She smiled at him and held out her hand. He dropped his guitar to the ground and strode across his back garden, jumping the fence between the two cottages in one fluid movement.

David reached her and took her hand in his. Not one word was spoken.

The connection between them was sealed as a jolt of heat ran up Megan's arm. He looked down at her, and his dark gaze held hers for a long moment before he took her in his arms and held her tightly against him.

Relief coursed through her body as he embraced her as though he'd never let her go. Warmth radiated through her and her heart drummed in her chest. She quivered with the effort of suppressing the emotion clogging her throat and wrapped her arms around his back.

"I heard my song." She kept her voice soft and parted her lips as he lifted his head.

"I wrote it because I didn't know where to look for you." Holding her eyes with his dark gaze, his deep voice sent a shiver coursing through her.

"I know. That's why I came back."

Slowly his lips lowered to hers as though they had all the time in the world.

"I meant every word, you know." He murmured against her lips and the vibration of his words sent the warmth rushing lower. "I love you, Megan. I want you in my life, wherever we are."

His words filled her with joy and his touch drifted over her lightly; the sensation of intimacy held a promise of their future.

Chapter Twenty-Seven

Two languorous days passed exploring each other and finding out about the other. Most of the time was spent in bed in David's cottage. Megan hadn't even entered the McLaren cottage.

She shivered as a finger ran lazily down her back. Propped on her stomach with her hands beneath her chin, she drank in the sight of David lying beside her on the bed. The look he returned went straight to her heart, cementing the feelings and words they had shared over the past two days.

Megan reached across and tangled her fingers in David's hair, wrapping a curl around her finger. Rolling over onto her back, she pulled his head across to hers and slid her lips slowly over his.

"I still can't believe I found you so easily." She smiled as he deepened the kiss and she let his hair go as he lay beside her. His skin was warm against hers and his fingers trailed down her side. "It was meant to be."

"Hey, I was trying hard over here too," he said. "I wasn't going to give up. Alice told me I would find you." He raised himself up on one elbow. "You know I don't understand all this time slip stuff, but she said she was a part of us finding each other."

"Do you know where she ended up?" Megan wondered if David knew. He'd told her about Alice's trip to the hospital and her insistence on staying back in 1971.

"No, I often wondered. She's never come back through the slip in the summers I have visited here. I've not seen anyone in her cottage until a particularly beautiful lady arrived a few weeks ago."

Megan smiled sadly and touched his hand. "Beth told me. Alice passed away three years ago and she's buried in the small cemetery in the village."

David looked away and stared towards the window for a while. "She must have been close to eighty?"

"Yes, she lived to a fine age. I'm sure Beth and her family have no idea about the stones and her travels. She kept herself very private and lost contact with them as she got older. The cottage is the only remaining link to her." Megan turned her head towards him and held his gaze. "A bit like a reclusive

281

rock star I was in love with when I was a teenager. Very private."

"No more travelling through stones?"

He nodded. "I have to go back to do some promotion for this album, and a couple of tours. Then for a few more albums and in about ten years for a reunion. Bear died in the eighties." He leaned over and kissed her briefly. "Come on, lazybones. We've got a visit to make. Time to get up."

Megan squealed as he slapped her bare bottom. Long legs and a sexy naked butt disappeared into the small bathroom and the shower began to run. He was right; they had a visit to make, but she'd join him in the shower first. She slid out of bed and followed him into the bathroom.

By the time they walked through the village and passed the Abbey, the sun was low in the western sky. They'd stopped at the village store and chatted to Jules as they'd bought a bunch of flowers to take with them. Streaks of pink and gold surrounded the low hills around them as David pushed open the gate to the small cemetery behind the Abbey. The air was still and quiet and a mystical sense enveloped them as they walked between the headstones.

"I'm sure she knows we got together." David crouched beside a simple black marble plaque and

282

read the words. "Alice Elizabeth McLaren, d. 10 November 2008. No birth date?"

"Beth said that was in her will. She stipulated there was to be no age on her plaque and they couldn't understand why but they respected her wishes."

"She was a sweet lady." David stood and wandered over to another grave and Megan followed him and placed the last of the flowers next to the simple wooden cross.

"Bear was a good man, too."

As they turned to leave the grave, a flash of light lit the sky and highlighted the three stone markers ahead of them. David took Megan in his arms and kissed her.

"We'll go home through the village, just in case."

Megan smiled and closed her eyes as his warm lips stayed on hers. "As long as we're together, Davy Morgan, it's home."

Epilogue

6 months later

David was sitting beside Megan on Tony and Kathy's deck overlooking the sparkling waters of Sydney harbour. Megan had come back to Australia to pack up and head home with him.

Home—to his island in the Caymans, but he had promised regular trips down under to visit the new baby sleeping in the pram beside Kathy.

"So where's the wedding going to be held?" Kathy asked as she leaned into the pram and picked up baby Jack.

Megan looked at her sister with a smile. "David has offered to fly you all to his island. We were thinking of a Christmas wedding in the Bahamas."

Tony nodded. "As long as little Jack here is up to a long flight, that sounds fabulous."

Megan jumped up as the doorbell rang. "Beth's here!" David watched as she hurried inside to answer the door.

A young woman with long blonde hair had her arm through Megan's when she reappeared. They were both smiling as Megan led her friend across to the table.

"Beth, this is David."

David stood and held out his hand." Hello, Beth. It's good to finally meet you."

"You too," Beth replied. "I've heard so much about you from Megan. And Megan said that you met my Aunt Alice briefly before she passed away."

"I did. She was a sweet old lady." David swallowed. It still made him nervous, wondering if his dual life would ever be discovered. The further he and Megan were from the stones in Glastonbury, the happier he was.

"I never met her, but my mother remembers her as a bit of an old hippie."

David simply smiled.

Beth turned back to Megan, excitement in her voice. "And I have news."

"I'm going to England and I'm going to live in Aunt Alice's cottage for a few months."

David and Megan looked at each other. "That's…um, exciting," Megan said. "But what on earth are you going to do in a cottage way out in the country for a few months?"

"I'm finally going to write that book I've been talking about for the last couple of years." Beth's eyes were bright. "And I've got the perfect plot. Mum found a trunk when she was over there, and it was full of Aunt Alice's diaries."

"Plot?" Megan's voice was so soft, David barely heard her question. "What sort of plot?"

He stood still as he waited for Beth to answer.

"Paranormal," she said with a smile. "If I told you what was in Aunt Alice's diaries, you'd never believe it."

THE END

Beth's story, *Follow Me,* continues this time travel series set in Glastonbury.

Alice's story is *Finding Home*

Laura's story is *The Threads that Bind*

You can find all of the buy links for the sequel here:

https://www.annieseaton.net/come-back-to-me.html

OTHER BOOKS from ANNIE

Whitsunday Dawn

Undara

Osprey Reef

East of Alice (November 2022)

Porter Sisters Series
Kakadu Sunset
Daintree
Diamond Sky
Hidden Valley
Larapinta

Pentecost Island Series
Pippa
Eliza
Nell
Tamsin
Evie
Cherry
Odessa
Sienna
Tess

Also available in three boxed sets
Books 1-3
Books 4-6
Books 7-10

The Augathella Girls Series
Outback Roads
Outback Sky
Outback Escape
Outback Wind
Outback Dawn
Outback Moonlight
Outback Dust
Outback Hope

Sunshine Coast Series
Waiting for Ana
The Trouble with Jack
Healing His Heart
Sunshine Coast Boxed Set

The Richards Brothers Series
The Trouble with Paradise
Marry in Haste
Outback Sunrise
Richards Brothers Boxed Set

Bondi Beach Love Series

Beach House
Beach Music
Beach Walk
Beach Dreams
The House on the Hill

Second Chance Bay Series

Her Outback Playboy
Her Outback Protector
Her Outback Haven
Her Outback Paradise
The McDougalls of Second Chance Bay Boxed Set

Love Across Time Series

Come Back to Me
Follow Me
Finding Home
The Threads that Bind
Love Across Time 1-4 Boxed Set

Bindarra Creek

Worth the Wait
Full Circle
Secrets of River Cottage (Nov 22)

Four Seasons Short and Sweet

Ten Days in Paradise
Follow the Sun

Others

Deadly Secrets
Adventures in Time
Silver Valley Witch
The Emerald Necklace
Christmas with the Boss
Her Christmas Star
An Aussie Christmas Duo (the two Christmas novellas)

About the Author

Finalist for the NZ KORU award 2018 and 2020.

Winner ...Best Established Author of the Year 2017 AUSROM

Long listed for the Sisters in Crime Davitt Awards 2016, 2017, 2018, 2019

Finalist in Book of the Year, Long Romance, RWA Ruby awards 2016

Winner ...Best Established Author of the Year 2015 AUSROM

Winner ...Author of the Year 2014 AUSROM

Best Established Author, Ausrom Readers' Choice 2017

Book of the Year (Whitsunday Dawn) Ausrom Readers' Choice Awards 2018

Annie lives in Australia, on the beautiful north coast of New South Wales. She sits in her writing chair and looks out over the tranquil Pacific Ocean. She has fulfilled her lifelong dream of becoming an author and is producing books at a prolific rate.

She writes contemporary romance and loves telling the stories that always have a happily Ever after. She lives with her very own hero of many years and they share their home with Toby, the naughtiest dog in the universe, and Barney, the rag doll kitten, who hides when the grandchildren come to visit.

See her latest releases on her website: http://www.annieseaton.net

If you would like to stay up to date with Annie's releases, subscribe to her newsletter here: http://www.annieseaton.net

Made in the USA
Columbia, SC
18 September 2024

42533923R00176